Mr Gunn

Tyler Hatch

A Black Horse Western

ROBERT HALE · LONDON

© Tyler Hatch 2013
First published in Great Britain 2013

ISBN 978-0-7198-0703-9

Robert Hale Limited
Clerkenwell House
Clerkenwell Green
London EC1R 0HT

www.halebooks.com

The right of Tyler Hatch to be identified as
author of this work has been asserted by him
in accordance with the Copyright, Designs and
Patents Act 1988

Typeset by
Derek Doyle & Associates, Shaw Heath
Printed and bound in Great Britain by
CPI Antony Rowe, Chippenham and Eastbourne

CHAPTER 1

DEAD MAN'S BOOTS

It was about as close to Hell as you could get without dying first.

Some claimed it was the biggest artillery barrage of the Civil War, or any other for that matter.

It was certain that the Yankees used their biggest guns, siting them almost two miles away, so that terror and bloody slaughter rained down out of the sky without warning.

But the sky was soon obliterated by the thick pall of powder smoke from the endless, overlapping explosions, and the shattered, burning timbers of the flimsy buildings that had once housed the long-suffering prisoners; the very weight of the swirling smoke pressed down on the carnage like some huge, flung cloak trying to hide the horror.

There were 217 Johnny Rebs living in that prison compound – plus barracks for thirty Yankee guards – when the barrage began.

When it ended there was only one man still alive, his naked flesh burned where the rags that passed for clothes had been seared from his rangy body by the heat and violence of the explosions. *What kind of freak luck had protected him?*

A blast like some giant hand had snatched him from where he lay prone, hands covering his head, and spun him end-for-end like a bone tossed to a dog before depositing him in a small depression ten yards away. He lay there, semiconscious after his head struck a rock, senses savagely assaulted by the constant conflagration that filled his world. It was the day when the very Earth itself shook.

The only way he knew that it was over was by the blurred sight of shattered bodies strewn around the massive butcher's shop that the compound had become; no longer was it being torn apart by the eruption of falling shells blasting the earth. Now it just steamed and smoked, without a single human voice raised in protest or crying for help that would never come.

His hearing had gone: there was nothing but a continuous high-pitched shrieking filling his head. His brain felt loose in his throbbing skull; his fingers were torn and bleeding where they had clawed into ground that he could still feel trembling through his belly and chest. His face was wet but he didn't know whether it was blood or tears from when he had screamed in mad defiance at the unseen cannon: *Stop! Stop! Stop!*

Why had they done it? The words sounded in his mind only: there was no real sensation of him shouting. Still, it was a good question! The long war was virtually over. Yet these *maniacs* had slaughtered all the prisoners in this hell-hole. Why? In some desperate attempt to cover up the inhuman brutalities that had occurred here? Kill all the witnesses so no one would ever know? They had almost succeeded; they had killed all but one: *him*!

He was sitting up now in his dusty depression, only vaguely aware that it had actually protected him from the fiery onslaught. It took long, long minutes for him to stand, nausea staggering him, his head spinning, as he cautiously looked around from his swaying height of six feet.

The shock of what he saw kicked his legs from under him and he fell sprawling, his mind refusing to accept the blood and shattered bodies that stretched away to the horizon.

His horizon was restricted by the slowly lifting curtain of roiling smoke and dust. Slowly, the overwhelming carnage was revealed.

He retched, hugged his bony chest, felt some of his own blood making his flesh slippery. His teeth chattered. His entire battered body quivered from head to toe. He was *freezing*. He looked wildly around for something warm to cloak his naked flesh – Hell! There were clothes aplenty! Many were just piles of shredded, smouldering, bloody rags, but some still remained miraculously intact, scattered like a crazy woman's laundry day.

He threw up when stepping cautiously among the raw meat of the corpses, tugging at this jacket or those trousers, a bloodstained shirt with a small rent in one sleeve. In time, he was dressed – except that his blistered, calloused feet were still bare. But there were plenty of boots to choose from. His throat constricted when he finally found a pair about his size in reasonable condition, still laced on a dead man's feet – no legs above the ankles – just a pair of mutilated feet, horribly encased in leather.

After recovering the boots he let his heaving stomach settle again and looked around for a coat of some kind; he was still cold. There was a mostly clothed Yankee officer, one of many amongst the dead guards or other prison staff who had been unfortunate enough to be on duty when hell rained down from the skies. The tunic was in fairly good condition, slightly torn in only a couple of places. It bore a captain's shoulder tabs but they didn't even register with him. He just slipped gratefully into it: it was a reasonably snug fit. He held it across his chest, fingers still too sore to fumble with the brass buttons, only three of which were still attached.

He huddled in a foetal position, engulfed by a powerful fear reaction. Later, he found himself sitting up, knees drawn up to his bearded chin, sucking down great gulps of air, trying to steady his thundering heartbeat as his fingers idly tugged at blood-matted hair on the back of his head.

Thoughts swirled like leaves in a whirlwind through his reeling mind. He muttered gibberish, shouted a few times, then realized his hearing was coming back – partially at least. He could hear his own shocked epithets as he condemned the perpetrators of this atrocity.

He clearly heard his own utterly despairing cry that was wrenched from him, futilely, as it slowly sank into his throbbing brain that he was the only living thing in the midst of this dreadful slaughter.

His mind simply could not retain the details of his ordeal. A blinding blade of light knifed into his tortured brain an instant before, mercifully, everything went black.

'Cap'n! Cap'n! You all right, sir?'

'You speaking to me, Sergeant?'

The lean soldier, down on one bent and bony knee, glanced up swiftly at the sound of Captain Murray's voice.

'Er . . . no, sir. I was . . . speakin' to . . . him.'

A dirty thumb indicated the body of a man with thick, blood-sticky hair and a beard clogged with all kinds of filth, lying at the edge of a tangled pile of shattered bodies. His dirty, torn tunic bore captain's bars on the shoulders.

'He's breathin', sir,' the sergeant added quickly as his senior officer frowned. 'I heard him moanin' and. . . .'

Captain Derrin Murray's jaw dropped. He was a career officer, in his mid-forties perhaps, and his somewhat rugged good looks were obvious even beneath the grime of long and hard riding that spattered his face, clogging his thin moustache beneath the classic Roman nose. Eyes that had seen a hundred battlefields with thousands of dead men narrowed as he swiftly knelt beside his sergeant, looking incredulous.

'He's – alive? In all this?' He swept an arm about him,

not looking at the mangled bodies, only at the slowly twitching whiskers of the beard on the face of the man sprawled before him. As he spoke he probed under the matted hair and found the neck artery. 'Good God Almighty! His heart is still beating!'

Murray twisted, calling for the medical corpsmen, remembering how he had grumbled back at Fort Allison that medics would be the last men needed at the site of the prison camp, known only as *Sierra Five* on the Army's books, and marked for obliteration.

'Goddammit! If those corpsmen don't get up here pronto they'll need some of their own kind to surgically remove my size-nine boots from their asses!'

Two hard-breathing, blood-spattered medics came rushing up, jostling to get at the unconscious man, eager to avoid Murray's wrath. The blond corpsman looked up sharply, blinking.

'By God, sir! His heart beats strongly, though somewhat erratically!'

'He deserves every chance we can give him, Cap'n,' said the second medic. 'To survive this! Why, it's a miracle.'

Murray glared. 'Rig a tent – and I want someone attending him all through the night. Understand? Every blamed minute!'

Their 'Yessirs' were not very enthusiastic but he knew they would obey.

They knew better than not to.

It was well after dark when he regained some form of consciousness: he didn't seem to be totally here, wherever here was. He felt as if he was standing slightly to one side, trying to join the reality and not quite managing it.

The tent was behind a boulder field that shielded the shambles of the prison compound from the campsite Murray had set up. The troopers who had accompanied him on this inspection were working by the light of campfires, trying to cover the evidence of the terrible barrage.

Eyes the colour of blued steel stared out from under clogged lashes as Captain Murray leaned close to the canvas stretcher where the survivor lay.

'Trust you're feeling better, Captain Landis?'

The man, partly cleaned up, his beard and hair scissor-cut closer to his features, a dressing on his head wound, tried to raise his head, but pain gripped him; he grunted and fell back. He coughed rackingly, body convulsing with the explosive efforts to clear his lungs. Those around him couldn't understand his first words: his voice was thickened, gravelly, his throat and air passages seared by the smothering smoke immediately following the barrage.

Sergeant Killen made out one word. 'I think he said "who", Cap'n. What're you trying to say, sir?'

The man tried very hard to speak clearly, had another fit of coughing, which shook his lean frame. He began to gulp and finally vomited into a bowl, hastily produced by the medic.

After he had rinsed his mouth with water, gnarled and blistered hands shaking, he cleared his throat. His red-dened eyes were wild, but they understood him when he asked, 'I know you?'

Murray smiled crookedly. 'No, sir.'

'Then . . . how you know . . . my . . . name?' His voice was raspy again and he spent half a minute trying to clear his throat. He spat as Murray said,

'The embroidered label in your tunic. The one your wife, I believe, sewed in: *This tunic belongs to Captain Burton Landis, husband of his loving wife, Beth.* You recall now, Captain?'

The pain-filled eyes wavered and he slowly nodded, wincing again as an obvious spasm caught his wrenched neck. 'Of course . . . my dear Beth!' he whispered slowly.

'I think he should rest some more, sir,' the corpsman said deferentially. 'It seems his memory is not too badly affected. A little more sleep and, well, he would be better able to manage any kind of . . . interrogation.'

Captain Landis swivelled his eyes from Murray to the medic, picking up on the latter's caution as he offered advice,

'You're probably right, Carson,' Murray allowed and the corpsman looked relieved. 'Give him a sleeping draught or whatever you think best and let him get some rest. The poor devil's earned it.'

He turned to add something more but bit back whatever words he had been about to say.

Captain Burton Landis was already asleep.

But Murray couldn't help thinking: the very last thing they expected – or wanted – was a damned survivor.

12

CHAPTER 2

DEAD AGAIN

They had moved him during the night.

Even as he noticed this in the biting chill of daybreak, he realized that the echoes of the terror-filled scream bouncing around inside his skull must have been of his own making: a result of some hideous nightmare.

There was no tent sheltering him now. He was lying on a handful of cut branches from one of the few surviving trees, lower down the slope. Turning his head, he saw uniformed men rushing towards his position, drawn by his waking scream. Beyond them the horror had suddenly become real. The slaughterhouse he had hoped was only a bad dream, he now saw was a reality.

Suddenly, once more there came the dull thud that had wakened him and evoked his scream: the sound of an explosion! *Nooooooooo!* his mind had shouted within his buzzing skull. Surely to God it wasn't starting up again?

Then there was the lean man in a sergeant's uniform

standing over him, a cocked pistol in his hand, the barrel pointing at his head and, shocked, he knew how it was going to be.

'What the hell, Cap'n?' asked Sergeant Killen, a little breathless, but because of the altitude rather than his exertions from the short run uphill after he'd heard the scream. 'Yellin' like that, you scared me white!'

The bearded man at the soldier's feet jumped as there came yet another dull explosion. Killen smiled thinly as he squatted, moving his gun slightly now. *So that was it!*

'Easy, Cap'n. The big barrage is finished. That's just some of the boys moppin' things up, blasting a few rocks loose here an' there, before riggin' the slide.'

The reddened, puzzled eyes stayed locked in the direction of Killen's tough face. 'S-slide?'

Killen glanced around him, waving back the other troopers who had started upslope when the man they knew as Captain Landis had cried out. He leaned closer.

'Cap'n, I'll tell you somethin'. It ain't gonna do you any good whether you know or not, see? It's like this: the big barrage was s'posed to totally obliterate Camp Sierra Five. The theory was all them shells bustin' up the camp would shake loose the permanent snow up there on the ridge and set it slidin'. Its weight would tear loose some of the surface boulders an' once they started rollin' the whole damn mountain face would slide an'. . . .' He paused, swept his arms out wide, 'come down and wipe out whatever was left of the camp, bury it under a couple thousand tons of rock and dirt. "Never existed", should anyone ask. You savvy?'

Dark, uncomprehending eyes stared up at him. Killen

nodded. 'Yeah, OK. You ain't right in the noggin' yet, which I been tryin' to tell Cap'n Murray, but he says orders is orders. No survivors, prisoners or our own boys who were guardin' 'em. Tough, huh? But there's gotta be no sign of any camp that might stir up God only knows what kinda trouble for the Reconstruction. So, you're just gonna have to,' he chuckled at the thought that he was about to put into words – '*go along with it*! You know what I mean?' He could hardly speak from the effort of trying to hold his laughter in. 'Go – along – with it! Get it? The whole damn mountainside'll be goin' down – and you and the big butcher's shop'll go with it. Nah? Don't get it?' He spat. 'Aaaah! You damn officers! None of you've got a sense of humour!'

He growled the last words, then jumped upright as Captain Murray came panting up the slope.

'Don't waste a bullet on that man, Sergeant!' Murray snapped as Killen raised his pistol. 'I believe now he may not belong to that tunic. Condition of his feet, hair and that beard . . . I think he was a damn prisoner! Either way, he should've died.'

Killen, still hunkered, let his his gun dangle loosely in his grip. 'How come the barrage didn't start the landslide like they said, Cap'n?'

Murray shrugged. 'Reckon they sited their cannon too far off. Can't blame the gunners for laying down their barrage too short: they just couldn't shoot any closer. Well, start the demolition team placing their charges. Sooner we get done, sooner we can get off this damn mountain.'

Murray glanced down and found himself looking into

the black depths of Captain Landis's eyes.

'Sorry about this, Landis.' He didn't sound 'sorry', just mouthed the words. 'Like to let you live after what you been through, but – you know politics. Or come to think of it, mebbe you don't. Fact is, this camp is a blot on our record, and now peace has come, we got the whole damn world watching us to see what kind of a job we're gonna make of building the new U-nited States of America. Means we can't afford to have anything known about places like this, if we're gonna put the bite on 'em for a few thousand dollars.'

Landis's gaze never wavered. He seemed as if he was gathering himself to say something but a bout of coughing shook him.

'It's OK if everyone knows about the Rebs and *their* slice of hell they called Andersonville: that'll get the world's back up agin the bastards. But we Yankees, we gotta come out clean as that there snow way up on top of the sierras. We need the backin' of foreign countries to get us on our feet, see? No one'd want to help us if they found out we had this horror camp for our prisoners of war. Now, you relax, try to get some sleep?' He smiled crookedly and added, 'It won't really matter if you don't wake up.'

Then, suddenly there was a small cyclone rearing up from where 'Landis' lay: Killen yelled in shock as clawed hands snatched the pistol from him, swiped him across the head and turned the weapon on Captain Murray. The captain stood there, frozen, mouth slightly open, staring at this wild-eyed man, now on his knees, menacing him with a cocked gun.

16

There was some guttural sound that he couldn't make out but he caught a few words: '. . . ain't gonna kill me!'

'Now wait a minute! Just wait!'

He was swaying now and Killen figured it was a good chance to nail him. He lunged suddenly.

Murray turned abruptly and started back down the slope. Killen tried to stop his own charge as the gun swung towards him. It fired.

Sergeant Killen's head snapped back and he spun away, sliding down the slope. The dazed man with the gun turned sharply, then fell, hearing Murray yelling for someone to shoot him down. He fell but he was on top of a small ridge now and had enough sense to kick hard, rolling his body across.

Then he couldn't stop – sliding, rolling, thrashing down to God knew where.

But wherever it was, it went abruptly dark.

It was a strange world he inhabited: a place he knew, yet didn't; he'd been here before, but couldn't remember when, or what had happened to him.

Yet he knew he was going to die, though he felt he had already died before this.

Throw all those things together and you had a mighty uncomfortable feeling that wasn't made any easier by the sounds of small explosive charges coming from many different directions: above, below, both sides. Then a strange, loud thunder and he felt the ground tremble and his belly knotted like a prize fighter's fist; his body prickled with a sweeping wave of oncoming terror.

'It damn well *is* starting again!'

He didn't know he had said the words aloud – and quite clearly if there had been anyone to hear. But he was alone on this bleak slope, a teetering mountain peak that rained dirt and rocks and – by Godfrey – some snow!

All these impressions suddenly coalesced in his thudding mind: he knew he had been through one inferno and now a second one was starting. Only this time, he would be buried under an entire damn mountain!

The thought was clear: his mind opened and grasped the significance immediately. The self-preserving instinct took over even as a huge amount of dirt and rubble swept over him. It might have taken his body with it if he hadn't been slammed against a rock. He thought his arching spine would snap.

It was almost full daylight now but the clouds of dust and raw, lung-tearing smoke were rapidly darkening the whole scene. By now, he was toppling and yelling, hurting, glimpsing what awaited him.

Off to one side most of the mountain slope was moving; the whole land seemed to be in upheaval, like water, surging, breaking up into islands of rocks and small trees, a monstrous tidal wave of dirt-streaked snow. And *noise*, so tangible it flailed his ears, resounded inside his skull.

Suddenly he realized that *he* was the one moving!

Yes! He was up on hurting feet, staggering, reeling drunkenly, but making a superhuman effort to reach one side of the slope. Although he didn't remember seeing it before, the arroyo must have registered somewhere in his battered mind and now, when life-threatening danger was imminent, his body had responded – hurled him

18

towards the only possible way out: the arroyo's edge. He couldn't believe he was coordinating so well, his legs were pumping and driving him away from the mountain top that teetered towards him.

A quick glance up. *Jesus!* Whatever was up there was blotting out the sky itself!

Later he would figure out that it was the entire peak of the mountain. Hell! The whole blamed peak had torn loose when the demolition team had blasted away the underpinning of boulders and steadying trees.

Suddenly he was flying.

That was his first impression, though the next instant he realized he must have hurled himself at the broken edge of the arroyo, which cut deep into the mountain on one side – the only side away from the path of the avalanche.

Bushes tore at him and he quickly got his hands up in front of his face, squeezed his eyes shut in his mad tumble. His body jerked and twisted and he yelled in pain as he was flung head over heels, upside down, pummelled on one side, wrenched back upright only to slam, full body-length into a sapling.

It had the give of young green, still-growing timber and bent under the impact. Like a bow it snapped erect again and he was flung like a missile into more brush that gave under his weight until he landed all atwist and tangled on soft ground, with the lower part of the bush growing only inches above his bleeding face. His lungs wheezed and popped as he struggled to draw in breathable air.

But he didn't know about that: these were instinctive

body reactions.

Then, as he heard the massive rumbling of the collapsing mountain, he was once more hurtled into a world that was totally black – yet strangely welcoming.

CHAPTER THREE

'MR GUNN'

The storekeeper wrapped the parcel in once-used brown paper and tied it with a short length of twine, plucked from a bundle he kept on a bent nail hammered in just under the edge of the counter on his side. A frugal man, but he had a warm smile and his store-bought teeth jiggled a little until a practised probing of his tongue settled the plate into a firmer position. When he walked he rolled like a ball – and had the figure to suggest as much.

'Young man, you are in my debt to the tune of three dollars and two bits. I hope you will not have to go hungry in order to settle up.'

The tall man across the counter set down the parcel he had been handed and dug deep into his faded, work-stained denim trousers. His hat was an old campaign cavalry affair with the brim floppy in one part, turned back in another, revealing a patch of thick fair hair above a scarred forehead and eyes that had the hard look of unpolished steel. But they softened as the man half-smiled, a little stubble rasping as he scratched with a calloused finger. He flicked those eyes down into the shorter storekeeper's face, pursed his lips and sniffed through narrow nostrils.

'I'm about forty cents short, storekeeper. Hey! Don't take the parcel back! Here's what I've got. . . .' He pushed a handful of change across. 'The rest I'll pay you in sweat: if you've got a chore worth forty cents that needs doin'.'

Haviland, the storekeeper, studied this obvious grubline rider briefly. Then he smiled again and went through the automatic ritual of settling his teeth firmly. 'Young man, your voice is kind of – rough, and I'm not sure I heard a'right. . . ?'

'You did. Show me some chore you want done that's worth forty cents – or mebbe a dollar and I'll take the sixty cents as pay and. . . .'

Haviland began to laugh, his big belly shaking under his floursack apron. He shook his head slowly.

'I am only glad you don't run a store in my town, mister! You are just a mite too smart for me! You owe me forty cents, yet you want to walk out of here with sixty cents of my hard-earned money in your pocket!'

'Leaving you a dollar's worth of muscle-power – and my debt paid. Sounds fair to me, *amigo*.'

Haviland's smile faded just a little; it was hard to tell for sure with this fellow's deep, raspy voice, as though something was clogging his throat, way back, but that *amigo* labelled him as a Southerner right off. But

Haviland was a fair man and the war had been over for some time now, so, shortly afterwards, the fair-haired man found himself stacking ten bags of sugar and four cases. Afterwards, he jingled sixty cents in his pockets as he picked up his parcel, tucked it under one arm and touched two fingers to his hatbrim.

As he reached the street door, Haviland said, 'You remember, now. Take the *narrow* trail past the Crouchin' Cat rock. It swings real sharp so you could miss it. It's the one you need to take you to that farm you was askin' about.'

'Obliged, again. This seems a friendly enough town. First I've come across in – well, some months.'

Then the door closed behind him and the store-keeper watched through a dirty display window as his late customer fixed his parcel to the saddle horn of a rig on a fine-looking roan gelding with a white patch on its left hip.

He swung up easily and settled into leather before he turned the horse, ready to ride out into the meagre traffic on Main Street, Climax, Colorado. It would take him in the direction of the Arkansas River, which he would cross, then continue on towards the distant Sawatch Ranges.

'Nice young feller,' Haviland remarked to his plump wife, who came in carrying a tray of newly bagged flour, ready for labelling. 'But he's got a kinda troubled look.'

'Something like the one you'll have if you haven't written out the labels for these bags yet!' She paused and rubbed her midriff, frowning. 'Oooh! I wish I could shake this nausea! I feel really queasy and jumpy.'

'Now try to control it, dear. Doc Howe says it's more in your mind than anything he can treat with medicine.'

'Beth Landis's medicine always works.'

'Yes, well, I don't plan on driving all that way for a spell. Oh-oh! There's Creedy and Devlin! Dammit!'

Haviland stiffened now as two men on foot ran up and deliberately stepped in front of the stranger's mount. The roan snorted as the rider hauled hard on the reins.

'Those two troublemakers! I saw them earlier looking at that feller's roan,' Haviland added worriedly.

The stranger calmed the horse, stared stonily at the two men: ex-Yankee soldiers judging by their ragged Union Blues.

Creedy was the bigger of the two, hard-faced, and he had a gun rammed into his belt; one hand rested on its butt. Devlin, shorter but powerfully built, swayed slightly, (Haviland thought: *Drunk as usual!*) then stuck his thumbs in his waistband, a strand of knotted rope. He wasn't wearing a gun, but there was a big Bowie knife in a worn leather sheath.

'Asked you earlier outside the saloon how you come by that there roan, feller,' Creedy drawled. 'You never did say.'

'No.'

Creedy shot a glance at Devlin. 'Hear that? Just one leetle word: "No!" an' I swear I can hear them darkies pickin' cotton in the background, hummin' away. That be right, Reb? Huh? How many slaves you have workin' for you?'

'None.' The stranger nudged the roan's flanks and the horse started forward. Devlin leapt at the bridle as

24

Creedy reached for his six gun.

The quiet stranger wrenched the roan's head savagely left, and its hard bony jaw caught Creedy across the side of the head, knocked him sprawling into the gutter. It startled Devlin and he froze in his efforts to lock his fingers around the Bowie's hilt.

The rider kicked his hand away. Devlin staggered off balance, but suddenly leapt up, catching the stranger off guard. The jarring impact unseated him; the horse whinnied as it jumped out into the street. The stranger fell awkwardly, and Devlin moved in, swinging a boot into his side. The stranger leapt up with a grunt, rammed the top of his head into Devlin's face. Creedy rushed in, pushing his dazed pard aside, ready to gunwhip the other man.

But he ducked and Creedy stumbled off balance, one leg going into the gutter. A fist like a riverboat's steam-driven piston knocked him out into the street where he lay, moaning, mouth bloody. Devlin charged back clumsily and the Johnny Reb easily ducked under the swinging fist, hooked him twice in the ribs, and slammed another blow to the temple.

Devlin joined his moaning, semi-conscious pard in the dust. The man mounted the roan, breathing hard, patted the tensed animal's neck and looked around at the small crowd that had gathered.

'I thought the War was over,' he said in his husky voice. 'A man's background ain't supposed to matter now.'

'That's right, feller,' called a hard-eyed man in bib-and-brace overalls. 'Long as he ain't a Reb!'

The crowd guffawed and some started forward. The

roan moved backward on command and Haviland came hurriedly out on to his porch.

'Here! You men stop this! He didn't start it. Creedy and Devlin braced him.'

'Cos he's a lousy Johnny Reb!' someone shouted.

'No. He's just a citizen, like the rest of us now. One country, one law for all.' Haviland took an almost pleading stance. 'Come on, gents! This is a good town. Let's keep it trouble-free. There's been enough bloodshed these past six years.'

'Save your breath, Granpaw! Your "citizen's" runnin' scared – like all his kind!'

The stranger was riding the roan down the middle of the street at a good pace, some of the crowd, loud in their protests, were calling insults after him.

The shopkeeper smiled thinly. 'You showed good sense, *amigo*!' he murmured to himself, turning back towards his store as Creedy and Devlin started to come round, clothes torn and dirty, and now a little bloody.

The trail was certainly narrow, the rider allowed silently as he worked the roan around the sharp rocks of the acute-angled bend, wincing as he knocked his left knee into a protruding piece of granite. The horse snorted as it, too, scraped its hide. Then they were around the big rock that resembled a crouching cat, and started down the steep grade.

He reined in when he got on to level ground, hooked a worn, spurless boot over the horn and built a cigarette from the dwindling supply of tobacco in the linen sack in his shirt pocket. When he'd lit up, he looked down and ahead through the heat haze of flat land. It rolled away into a partly seen vista of grass and at least two creeks and some patches of timber. Maybe he could glimpse a bend of the big river beyond.

There were small cabins dotted out there, like match-boxes, fence wire glistening in the sunlight, splitrail and lodgepole marking boundaries. The greenery of a vegetable garden drew his eyes to a couple of the cabins. Other set-ups were obviously for dairy cattle.

And beyond, way at the far end of the valley, he saw clouds of dust and a moving, rippling dark mass that could only be a herd of cattle being hazed by riders.

He paused with the cigarette halfway to his mouth, lips thinning a little.

Nesters and cattle ranchers sharing the same valley?

Not exactly a recipe for peace and harmony. Wouldn't take much of a spark to set off trouble in such a situation.

On that thought he settled into the saddle again and set the roan down the trail from the ledge.

Holding the reins in his left hand, letting the mount make its own way, he found his right hand brushing the scratched and worn butt of the revolver he wore on his right hip in a cut-down cavalry holster, minus the flap.

Trouble was the last thing he wanted, but if it couldn't be avoided he was ready. He remembered Creedy and Devlin as he nudged the roan forward. Had he told that storekeeper he thought Climax was a friendly town?

Something told him he had not come to Paradise.

He stopped by two farms before he got directions to the one he was after.

The man at the second place had been swinging an axe, trying to cut through the tough taproot of a large tree stump. He had a long way to go and the rider gestured to the pile of woodchips around the man's boots.

'You got another axe, we could have that stump out before sundown.'

The farmer stiffened, squinted, adjusted his old hat as he took a closer look at this stranger. 'You look like one of them Half-Moon riders to me.'

'Dunno no Half-Moon.'

'You still look like a cowpoke to me. Why would you offer a farmer help?'

The rider arched his eyebrows. 'If I had to fight a stump that tough, I'd be glad if someone offered me help, whoever he was.'

It was the farmer's turn to frown. 'Well, I'm obliged, I guess. It just ain't usual round here, is all.' Then, with a sudden nudge from his conscience, the farmer said, 'That well-water's mighty cool if you want to wash the dust outta your throat.'

The rider nodded, nudged the horse across to the well, where he dismounted. He drank a dipperful, poured some into his hat and let the roan drink too.

'You've got right cool water here, friend. Thanks.'

The farmer lifted the axe above his shoulder, ready for the next blow, paused, called, 'Name's Tom O'Malley.'

The rider lifted a hand in acknowledgement without turning – or giving his own name.

The place he was looking for wasn't exactly run down – but it was only a frog's leap from it.

Coming down the short rise into the hollow where the cabin was he noticed that several roof shingles lay skewed and lifted on one side. In a decent fall of rain you could wash in the parlour – if there was one. Which he doubted.

The front door was upright but the leading edge had gouged a mighty noticeable arc where it dragged across the ground hinges: needed adjusting, or renewing. There was only one window with glass in it and the pane was cracked in a crazy spider's web.

No man to tend to the chores, he allowed silently.

There was a neat, well-tended vegetable garden on one side of the doorway, and on the other a flower patch. He shook his head slowly. *Typical: some folk try to make a place look more presentable at the cost of wasting good fertile soil on flowers.*

Not the way to run a farm, he reckoned – then tensed as he stopped the roan in the cluttered front yard.

How the hell would he know that? He was no sod-buster . . . was he?

Just then a woman appeared in the doorway, using the sagging door to shield half of her body as she lifted a single-barrelled shotgun and pointed it in his general direction. She was dark-haired, pushing thirty, he judged, average size, maybe a mite on the skinny side. Her face, grim now, had good lines and her clothes, though clean, had seen a lot of wear.

'If you're one of Bryce McCall's Half-Moon men, you can turn right around and get off my land!' Her voice was pleasant enough but there was strain in it, and the way she held herself told him she was pretty damn tense and nervous.

'No, ma'am, I ain't from Half-Moon. I've come up from Climax, and way south of there to start with.'

She tossed her head so the dark hair that had fallen across part of her face was flicked aside. He saw her brown eyes narrow. The gun wavered slightly but if she pulled the trigger the spread of shot would still blow him out of the saddle.

'I thought I detected a touch of a Southern accent. You ought to be more careful.' At his brief frown, she added, 'You're a long way from home, Reb.'

His deep-tanned face stiffened, not with alarm or offence, but almost as if it was a thought that hadn't occurred to him. Or, if it had, it had made no impression on him. *It still don't*, he thought, then he tried a smile, his somewhat thin lips moving only slightly. 'You disappoint me, ma'am.'

'In what way?' The voice was edgy now: she was uneasy that her shotgun hadn't made him more . . . leery of her.

'Well, it's kinda disconcerting to come upon a nice-lookin' lady, such as yourself. . . .' He paused, licked his lips briefly, 'and have a shotgun stuck in your face. When all you're hopin' for, is for her to recogniz'e her own husband.'

Nothing seemed to change, yet somehow she looked more like a statue now, frozen into immobility, the brown eyes cold and maybe just a tad disappointed.

The long silence stretched. A shoo-fly buzzed through the doorway unnoticed. The roan stamped a hind foot and flicked its tail. A little sweat broke out on the man's sober face. Her narrowed eyes showed clearly against the marble of her skin, locked briefly on to his gaze, then shifted marginally as she said, very clearly, 'Well, this is a new twist, I have to admit, but surely your bunkmates have told you that my husband is dead!'

The rider was just as tense as she was and the tip of his tongue showed briefly between his suddenly dry lips. Hoarsely he said, 'Was he named Burton Landis?'

She swayed suddenly and the shotgun almost fell from her hands. He thought she was going to faint and started to dismount. Then the gun was in her grip again and this time she cocked the hammer, the butt rising to her shoulder.

'He – is – dead! He went missing two years before the end of the war and I have had unofficial notice since that they believe he died in a fierce battle going into the history books as "Hellfire Bend", in the Sangre de Cristo sierras. I am assured he conducted himself . . . heroically . . . so, yes, I am a widow, and I have no use for you stupid cowboys thinking I would want you anywhere near my bedroom. Under any circumstances.' Her head tossed, brown eyes challenging.

He was frozen halfway out of the saddle and said warily, 'I'd like to . . . step down all the way, ma'am.'

'Go ahead. But stand very still! Or, whoever you are, and whatever your intentions, I *will* shoot you.' Her breasts heaved with her deep, quickened breathing. He knew he had to be mighty careful or, in her rising excitement, she might well release that hammer.

He stood carefully beside the roan, making sure his right hand was well away from his holstered gun. 'You don't recognize me, then?'

31

The smooth brown skin between her eyes creased briefly. 'I've never seen you before in my life. Now what kind of stupid game are you playing? Your bunkmates must be fools, to think a Johnny Reb could pass for my husband!'

He heard the catch in her voice and lifted his hands quickly in a peaceful gesture.

'I guess I was kinda unthoughtful, there, ma'am. But I was told my name was Captain Burton Landis and – well, after driftin' around for some months, and comin' to Climax, I heard the Landis name and asked around. I was told you were the captain's wife. I – I 'm sorry if I upset you.'

'I don't know what you're talking about.' She was agitated now and he watched the knuckle of the finger she had on the shotgun's trigger. If it whitened at all, he was going to dive for the ground and hope for the best.

'And what d'you mean, you were *told* you are Burton Landis?'

Aloud he said, 'Actually, I'm called Mr Gunn.'

For an instant, after a hesitation, she relaxed slightly. 'Well, they'd hardly call you *Mrs* Gunn, would they?'

'It ain't quite the joke it seems, ma'am.' He paused, thinking out his next words carefully. 'You see, I was told I was Captain Burton Landis because I was wearing his tunic – which I have in my bedroll there – and I guess even though I was feelin' mighty poorly, I knew it wasn't really my name.'

He saw she was about to speak, utterly puzzled at what he was saying. He quickly added, 'I know it's confusing, but truth is, ma'am, I – I dunno *who* the hell I am – where

I've come from, where I've been, how I got to the place they called Camp Sierra Five. All of it is one big black blank. I was kinda hopin' you might help me.'

'Help you?'

'Right now, ma'am, I'm nothing. I got no home, no name. Not even this "Mr Gunn". That only came about because I took up with a wagon train of Dutch immigrants who were set on by renegades. I kept asking for a gun to help fight 'em off. 'Gimme a gun!' I yelled. 'I want a gun! I have to have a gun!' That kinda crazy thing, like it happens when there's action and no time to lose. Afterwards, 'cause I shot so many of the raiders and still didn't know my own name, they called me Mr Gunn. . . . Actually, *Mejnheer* Gunn in their lingo.'

She stared at him, not aware that she had lowered the shotgun. There had been quite a few men stop by this place since she had officially become a widow, and they had had all kinds of elaborate stories to tell, each devised to lead straight to her bed.

But this – this one's efforts seemed to be tying him in knots and it was about as crazy a thing as she'd ever heard. Still, she was intrigued, too. He said he had been wearing Burt's tunic! She knew little about her husband's death – and just as little about his life, come to that!

'I thought you might like your husband's tunic, ma'am. It ain't in the best of condition, but it may be somethin' to – remember him by.'

Suddenly she found herself fighting tears and stepping aside. She still kept the gun barrel slanting downwards. She cleared her throat.

'That was thoughtful of you. I guess you'd best come

in,' she invited, her voice somewhat hoarse, her heart thudding at her own temerity.

Or was she afraid of what she might learn about her husband?

Just who was this stranger, who *seemed* so thoughtful?

CHAPTER 4

BETH

The interior of the cabin was sparsely furnished but very clean, even the hard-packed earthen floor appeared to have been swept. There were no noticeable spillages staining the stones of the hearth at the open fireplace, nor any cobwebs on the underside of the shingled roof, either. A strange thought came into his mind: here were signs of a woman who was meticulous: naturally, or maybe forcing herself to be that way, just so as to keep busy, tire the body and mind so troubles that would not go away could be temporarily pushed to the back of consciousness by sheer exertion.

He had no idea where the thought came from: as far as he knew he'd never had one like it before. But how would he even know that? He judged he was about thirty years old, yet he had a memory that went back only a few months.

He sipped from the thick china cup she had set before

him. 'Good coffee.'

'I've only used the beans once before,' she said, a flush colouring her cheeks at the admission. She avoided his gaze across the table. 'I don't drink a lot of coffee.'

'Things're pretty tough all round these days.'

Her eyes took on a hard look as she turned her own cup between her hands. 'They are. And "Reconstruction" was supposed to make life a paradise for us all!'

'Not for Johnny Rebs. We're the losers, and never allowed to forget it.'

She sighed. 'Yes. It must be hard. Er . . . are you trying to disguise your Southern accent? I mean, your voice is unnaturally thick, very hoarse and I wondered if. . . ?'

He smiled crookedly, shaking his head. 'Woke up with it that way after the big barrage.' At her puzzled frown, he added, 'I have a memory of a mountain being blown apart, first by cannons, then – well, the whole blamed mountain seemed to collapse.' He lifted a hand at the incredulous look on her face. 'I'm not exaggeratin', ma'am. It's . . . well, I guess it's my first memory – the one where my present memory starts anyway.'

'I'm not sure I understand. 'She fidgeted uneasily.

He smiled inwardly, thinking *And not sure you should've invited me in, either!* Aloud, he said, 'Briefly, ma'am, I recall finding myself stark naked in the midst of hundreds of dead men on a mountain slope that'd been blasted to rubble by Yankee guns. Later I found I was wearing most of a Union uniform, includin' an officer's jacket I'd taken off a dead man. There was a sergeant kneelin' by me, callin' me "Captain" because there were captain's bars on the shoulders of the jacket. Another

Yankee – an officer, too – "Murphy" or some name like that – told me that a label inside the jacket said I was Captain Burton Landis.'

A hand went quickly to her mouth. 'My stars! It – it must have been Burt's body you took the jacket off!'

'I guess so. With the label – that's why they thought I was your husband. I dunno what happened next, but I came round in a ditch and the mountain had collapsed, buried all the dead men and smashed buildings that I could recall seein'. I did a heap of wanderin' after that, mostly afoot, and I've no real memory of it. Then I won that horse I got outside in a poker game and some drunken Yankee come after me with a gun; said the horse was his, rightfully, and he aimed to take it.'

He stopped speaking abruptly, then continued, 'Cut a long story short, ma'am, he took it and later I seen it at a hitchrail and. . . .' He shrugged, drained his cup. 'Like I said, I did a lot of wanderin', but I had me a horse and the name of Gunn. I had to dodge the Reconstruction squads. Found I could live off the land. Eventually I picked up on the Landis name in this area, and here I am. I'll bring you the tunic.' He started to rise but she shook her head, motioned him to stay seated.

'Not just yet.' She toyed with the cup and he let the silence drag on until she looked up and he saw there were tear marks down her cheeks. 'I suppose the dead man you took the jacket off had to've been Burt?'

'I dunno, ma'am, I'd like to say yes or no, but I just don't recall. I'd be inclined to think so, though, but that place was a long ways from Hellfire Bend.'

After a short while she got up and cooked him some

eggs, not speaking until she served them on a plate with two golden, crusty biscuits.

'I made the biscuits yesterday. But they're quite palatable.'

Around a mouthful, he said, 'Ma'am, you have no idea of some of the things I've had to eat and convince myself they were "palatable". If you've got some chores you'd like done, I'm willing to help out.'

She waved his offer away. 'If I start looking for chores that need doing, you'll be here for a week!'

Soberly he said, 'That's OK by me. I got nowhere special to go.'

Her eyes snapped to his face. 'I meant that jokingly.'

'I didn't. I dunno how or why, but I've found I'm pretty good as a handyman. Mebbe I had a small spread of my own, one time. . . .' His voice drifted off as he steered away from the oft-unbidden thoughts of what his past might have been.

She felt a sudden compassion for this man, surprised that she so readily believed his story. 'It must be very difficult not being able to recall your past.'

He merely nodded and took out his tobacco sack, pausing to gesture with it, arched eyebrows asking her permission to smoke at the table.

'Of course you may smoke. My name's Beth, by the way.' Then she put a couple of fingers to her lips, realizing he could not introduce himself in return. 'We don't really need to be formal.'

'Reckon I'm about as informal as you can get where names are concerned, Beth.' He smiled easily now and she thought it softened his face, which had been set in stiff lines of worry kept just below the surface.

'Well, can you think of a first name you'd like to go with Gunn?'

He shook his head. 'Gunn seems good enough.'

'I really didn't know much about Burt's army life,' she said abruptly. 'He let slip once that he was some kind of spy. That he went behind enemy lines, posing as a Southerner. He was originally a stage actor, and good at disguise and accents, you see, and I suppose that helped him carry off whatever role he was playing.'

The man calling himself Gunn rubbed hard at his forehead. 'I think I recall this Cap'n Murphy – no, that name's not quite right, but let it go. I seem to remember him sayin', on that mountain, that the way I looked, bushy hair and beard, feet all cut from not wearing boots, that I was more like a prisoner than a captain in the Union Army. And someone else, I think mebbe that sergeant who woke me, said he'd heard that Burt Landis might've been planted among the Rebel prisoners to gain their confidence and so pick up information that he could pass along to the camp commander.'

'You keep saying "camp"?'

'Yeah. It was a prison camp, called Sierra Five, a worse hellhole than the Rebs' Andersonville in Georgia. That's why the Yankees destroyed it, wiped it off the face of the earth, didn't want the world to know how they treated their prisoners. Victors or no – I still dunno how I got out alive. Or what I was doing there in the first place.'

'And Burt? He – died there? Not at some battle called Hellfire Bend?'

Gunn hesitated, then nodded curtly. 'Reckon so,

Beth. No one coulda got off that mountain alive.'

'You did,' she said softly, bringing a deep frown to his tortured-looking face.

He nodded. 'I've no idea how. I'm mighty sorry if you had hopes your husband was—'

'No!' She spoke sharply. Then, quietly, 'No. I – I've come to terms with the fact that Burt is dead. It's all right. I've lived with it long enough now not to come apart at the seams when I think about him and our life together. But, just why *did* you come here?'

He shrugged. 'I'm not sure. Guess mebbe I thought there was just a faint hope that I might've really been this Burton Landis, and there was some kind of life waiting for me to pick up where I'd left off. If not, I figured you might care to have his tunic: a kinda – remembrance.'

He tensed as she reached across the table and briefly squeezed his left hand with her slim fingers.

'I'm sorry that you don't even know your own name!' she said. 'Oh, it's too dreadful to contemplate. I suppose that's not news to you! I – I'm all a'fumble somehow, and . . . at a loss for words.'

He nodded jerkily. 'I'm obliged for your—'

He stood abruptly, cutting off whatever he was about to say. His hand groped for his gun and he tugged it from the holster.

'Riders!'he snapped, as he strode to the doorway. The woman followed. They looked past the sagging planks, across the meadow now turning a light golden colour as the afternoon sun sank lower towards the mountain crest.

Six or eight riders were coming in towards the cabin.

Their blue uniforms showed plainly in the clear light, as did the unsheathed rifles of at least three of the riders.

'Damn!' Gunn breathed with feeling.

Beth Landis frowned. 'But you have nothing to fear, have you?'

'Apart from being a Johnny Reb, you mean? Which is plenty bad enough, I'm beginning to find out. See those two riders in ragged clothes on the edge of that bunch? They picked a fight with me before I left town. I had to get kind of rough, left 'em both in the street, knocked out. My guess is they're not here to kiss and make up.'

CHAPTER 5

FUGITIVE

Gunn did not at first recognize Captain Murray (now Major, nor Sergeant Killen, now a lieutenant.)

There were three troopers with them, as well as Creedy and Devlin: these last two showing fresh gravel scars on their sour faces. The troopers were holding the unsheathed rifles that had caught Gunn's attention as the bunch rode in.

Murray introduced himself and Gunn nodded gently.

Yeah! 'Murray', not 'Murphy': the man who had tried to question him while he was lying more than half-dead on that mountainside, (as far as his current memory went).

But Gunn would have looked a heap different at that time: bushy, matted hair, beard halfway down to his waist, covered in filth and dried blood. Maybe Murray wouldn't recognize him.

'Who're you?' Murray demanded, almost echoing

Gunn's thought, swivelling his gaze from Beth to Gunn. 'I know you?'

Gunn shrugged. 'If you do, I dunno you.'

'The major asked you a question, Reb!' snapped Killen, heavy frontier moustache bristling as his lips stretched into taut lines. He dropped a hand to his holstered pistol.

'I answered.'

'You answer with respect when you address the major. You were asked your name.'

Beth covered the alarm she felt rising as she saw Gunn's mouth tighten and knew he was about to sass these men again, and get himself into even more trouble.

'He's my brother. Zachariah Gunn,' she blurted abruptly, the name just sliding into her mind. 'He's come to visit. We haven't seen each other in years.'

Killen curled his mouth in disbelief, but Murray arched his eyebrows beneath his campaign hat. 'You're admitting to being kin to a Reb, Mrs Landis?'

'Well, it's this way: we were born in Rockford, Illinois, but our parents split up. My father took the boys, Zack and another brother, Lance, since killed in the War, and went South. They were very young and I guess that's how come Zack has a hint of a Southern accent.'

Murray's gaze was steady, unreadable, but his voice was clipped. 'Good answer, ma'am, but it still makes him a Reb. He took up arms against the Union. We'll let it stand at that. Just as long as it's clear: he's a recent enemy of the Union.' He turned again to Gunn. 'In typical Reb fashion, you've bucked the Reconstruction laws and

43

attacked two men who're just trying to make decent lives for themselves again after surviving the hell of the war – on the Union side.'

'These two? They jumped me in Climax. No warning.'

'Hell, Major, he was ridin' my brother's hoss an' all I wanted to know was how he come by it! I'd already asked him once before but he just walked away. Ignorant, like all damn Rebs.'

'That's right, Major,' Devlin said, backing Creedy's story. 'Creedy's brother, Josh, won that hoss in a card game in Boulder. This damn Reb claimed the hoss was rightfully his an' stole it! But Josh must've put up a helluva fight 'cause they found him in a saloon alley, kicked to death.' He pointed to the roan horse standing with trailing reins a few yards away. 'That's Josh's hoss right there! You ask me, this damn Reb's guilty of murder!'

Gunn kept his face blank as Devlin waved a long accusing finger with a dirty nail at him.

'That's the way it happened, Major,' confirmed Creedy, getting worked up. 'Josh won that hoss. Next thing this damn Reb turns up ridin' it! – an' Josh is lyin' dead in some stinkin' alley in Boulder. I want justice here.'

'Seems you're in a lot of trouble, Gunn.' Murray shook his head slightly, glanced at the woman. 'Ma'am, I knew your husband and I respected the job he was doing, risking his life by mingling with those miserable prisoners in—' He stopped abruptly at a warning frown from Killen: he had been about to mention Sierra Five. The major cleared his throat.

'It's a long story and likely has nothing to do with the present one. Gunn, you're under arrest and you'll be taken in custody back to Fort Harlin. Your story'll be investigated and you may be brought to trial.' He lowered his voice and added, 'And if you're found guilty, you'll hang.'

Beth gasped, but quickly recovered. 'That's not fair! Nor even legal! You haven't heard Zack's side of the story yet!'

'He'll have his chance to explain during the hearing,' Murray said irritably. 'You'd be wise to keep out of this, Mrs Landis. While I'm willing to allow you a little leeway because of your husband, if you try to interfere with my duty in any way. . . . Well, I am a deputy commissioner for Summit County here, as you well know, and our laws apply to *everyone* living within my jurisdiction, Reb or Yankee.'

'They are damn harsh laws, Major!' Beth flared. 'I mean, you say you hold respect for my late husband. Well, this is – was – his place. I'm still his wife, a Northerner to boot, yet I'm hounded by your adminis-tration for taxes that I doubt are even legal! You've used them as an excuse to confiscate almost half of my land! Even takn my dairy cattle which I relied on for milk and butter. All because I couldn't raise the money on time!'

'Careful, Mrs Landis!' Murray sat straighter in the saddle, jaw thrusting, eyes cold. 'You are making what can be construed as seditious talk against the Reconstruction.'

'Oh, I know what powers you have! You enforce them often enough.'

'Perhaps it's time I enforced some of them again! This is—' He stopped abruptly as one of the troopers swore. Listening to the major argue with the woman, all three had relaxed and unconsciously lowered their rifles. Now they found themselves covered by a cocked pistol in Gunn's hand.

'Leave her be! She's got a legitimate complaint.'

The major's eyes narrowed. 'That pistol only holds five rounds. There are seven of us – or can't you count!'

Gunn smiled for the first time, a cold, twisting movement of his lips that brought more than a tad of worry to the faces of the Union men. 'You want to draw straws to see who survives? If I've got five shots, Murray, you go first. I won't be playing favourites, just shooting till my gun's empty. There'll be five of you dead, believe me. I'm a good shot and this range is barely more than arm's length.'

'Zack!' gasped Beth, her face twisted in concern. 'I think this is only making things worse.'

He smiled faintly and she bit her lower lip. He was playing out a bluff to the limit: but he had put himself in a mighty bad position.

'So, gents, let those rifles slip to the ground. That's it. Killen, get rid of your guns. Murray, you toss your pistol down the well, seein' as you're so close.'

Beth was shaking, her eyes flitting from one man to another, as they reluctantly obeyed. Gunn climbed aboard the roan with the white patch, his gun still covering the others, who were now on foot. He nudged the roan forward, leaned down and gathered the trailing reins of the posse's mounts.

'OK, gents. Start walkin' into the sundown, and keep on going. I'll be able see your silhouettes for a long time and I've got all these rifles to pot-shot at anyone who tries to make a break for it. Git movin'. *Now!*'

They hesitated but started walking. Murray's face was white with fury, Killen's mouth was set in a tight line. The troopers just walked, used to obeying orders whatever they might be. Devlin and Creedy shuffled along, Creedy growling:

'You better kill me now, Reb! I won't forget what you done to my brother. He raised me from a shaver an'—'

'Just keep walking, Creedy. Or I'll shoot you in the leg and *still* make you walk.'

'You realize you're a fugitive as of this moment?' asked Murray in clipped tones, eyes blazing. 'We'll get you, don't think we won't. And when we do, you'll hang.'

'Then I'd have nothing to lose by shooting you all right now.' Gunn lifted the revolver and the troopers stared, drop-mouthed. Murray and Killen stiffened. Creedy and Devlin looked as if they might make a last-second dive for the ground, but were mighty leery.

'*Don't!*' cried Beth in alarm, whitefaced.

Gunn shook his head. 'No. I need my bullets, which makes 'em lucky. Just light out for that horizon. *Pronto!*'

Twenty minutes later they were well clear of Beth's boundary; small hurrying, staggering figures against the sundown fire. Tensely, Beth turned to the closely watching Gunn, now with a Spencer rifle in his hand. She sounded somewhat breathless when she said:

'You don't realize what you've done, do you?' He

47

stared, frowning slightly. 'Oh, you might *think* you know how hard Reconstruction can be, but you don't *know*! You'll be hunted relentlessly. Very few men who are classed as "Rebel outlaws" ever escape the death penalty. They'll never give up.'

'Then I have to thank you doubly for the way you spoke up and said I was your brother. Fast thinkin', and it was a mighty brave thing to do.'

'Foolish, more like,' she said with a trace of bitterness. Then there was a touch of a smile. 'I'm sorry I burdened you with Zachariah.'

'Shortened to Zack it's OK.'

'This – this must be awfully difficult for you, I mean, your lack of memory and so on. You realize you could come up against a mortal enemy and not even recognize him?'

He nodded and she saw by the way his mouth tightened that he was fully aware of such a risk. There was nothing he could do about it, of course. He knew that sometime – any time – he might have to face such a situation.

'Where will you go?'

'There's a whole country out there I don't remember ever seeing. Mebbe something'll jog my memory.'

'Oh!' She shook her head briefly, plainly at a loss as to what to say.

He smiled wryly. 'Beth, I'm obliged for everything. I just hope this doesn't kick back on you. I mean, leaving you to face whatever Murray can come up with to hassle you.'

She waved his words aside and, looking directly at

him, ventured: 'I have to ask—'

'About Creedy's brother?' He shook his head. 'No. I didn't kill him. I was just drifting through town and saw the roan tied to a saloon hitchrail. It was dark, and quiet, so I mounted up and decided to cut through the alley beside the saloon, keep off the street, you know?'

He paused, shaking his head slowly. 'Just my luck Josh was there, doing up his trousers' front. I could smell the booze on him. He must've recognized me or, more likely, the horse. He grabbed for his six-gun and jumped at me. The horse veered away but I kicked out at the gun. I missed and my boot hit him in the face. He went down and I jumped the horse over him and lit out pronto. He was scrabbling around, searching for his gun when I cleared the alley. He never shot at me so I guess he didn't find his gun – or whoever kicked him to death found it. But after I'd gone. That's gospel, Beth.'

She held his gaze and slowly nodded; she knew instinctively that he was telling the truth.

He added, quietly, 'Earlier, when I hit town, I had a couple of dollars and bluffed my way into a poker game. I got lucky and won. But the loser had no cash left and he'd put up the horse for the bet. So I took the horse in payment.'

'Where does Josh Creedy fit in?'

'He was in the game too; hit the bottle hard, dropped off to sleep and missed a hand or two. Claimed I'd doped his likker. Showed me some gold disc he had on a leather thong round his neck. Claimed it was his luck-piece and never, ever let him down. So, to his mind, he *had* to've won and I had to be stealing what was rightfully his. He was still drunk – or loco, more like, with that kinda reasoning. Wild-eyed and rarin' to kill, the damn fool.'

She looked at him thoughtfully. 'Are you one of those unfortunate people who attract trouble?'

He smiled wryly. 'Wish I knew.'

His answer brought a flush to her cheeks. She said abruptly, 'Step inside and I'll draw you a map of a place where you'll be safe. It's hidden by a small waterfall – no, don't argue, Zack.' She turned and stepped into the cabin, lighting a lamp before he followed. She took an old store bill and began to draw on the back. 'Just ride and put as much distance as you can between Reconstruction and yourself.'

'I aim to.'

She handed him the crudely drawn map and pointed out landmarks, ticking each as she did so. 'We're here. You ride south-east to the edge of the foothills, swing into the ranges right about here, beyond a boulderfield where most of the rocks have a cap of scaly moss.'

When she had finished he folded the map into his shirt pocket. 'What've I got to lose? No past that I can remember, no future I can foresee. But I'm still a mite anxious about you being here alone, Beth.'

Looking mildly embarrassed, she said quietly, 'Well don't be. I already have a sort of protector.'

He gave her a puzzled frown.

'A man named Lobo McRae. He was Burton's sergeant, with him in the battle where Burton went missing. But he survived and came back to watch out for me. He – er – had been trying to court me before I met Burton, actually.' She flushed. 'He still carries a torch for me, I think. He means well, though. I know he won't let any harm come to me, says he owes it to Burton who once saved his life. He has a small place up in the hills, comes down from time to time to check on me.' She smiled. 'I'll be all right, Zack. Truly.'

He saw no profit in standing around debating that. He touched a hand to his battered hatbrim as he nudged the roan forward.

'As some of us Johnny Rebs say, *muchas gracias,* and *hasta la vista.* I'll be seeing you.' He flicked a hand to his hatbrim as he rode away from the sundown, towards the thickening darkness of the valley and the wild country beyond.

CHAPTER 6

LOBO

The waterfall was actually a damn nuisance.

He had not found the niche in the hill that Beth had directed him to until almost sunup the morning after leaving her farm.

There had been a moon, but once into the hills he found they were unexpectedly tortuous and higher than they had seemed during the day. Shadows confused him and though the roan gave him no trouble he got lost more than once. When the horse stepped out of some waist-high grass and plunged belly-deep in a pool of scummy water, Gunn quit the saddle, got the horse ashore and broke a slim sapling. He walked on ahead then, holding the horse's reins loosely, prodding and testing the ground in front. It was slow – *damn* slow – but better than drowning in some swamp hole or stepping off a cliff.

Come sunup he rested on a ridge, took an estimate as

to the direction he was facing and sat down with his back against a deadfall, fumbling at his almost emtpy tobacco sack in his shirt pocket. The crude map Beth had drawn him crackled and he pulled it out, smoothed it over a bent knee and squinted at it in the growing light of sunrise.

'Ah, *shoot*!' he spat, cursing himself for an over-confident fool. He'd reckoned he could memorize the sparse details of such a hurriedly drawn map, had trusted that quick scan he had made of the sketch – and he had been wrong!

A symbol that he had taken to mean a big boulder was actually a tree as seen from directly above, a big blob of foliage and he hadn't noticed the hastily sketched trunk. Now he saw by another landmark, a broken peak, that he had come to the wrong side of the shattered crag.

And his remaining tobacco was too damp to smoke!

Calling himself every kind of a fool he could think of, he hastily mounted and got the roan moving. He had better be quick now, the day was dawning and looked like being hot and bright. Murray's men would be sure to be abroad.

So he came to the waterfall. He heard it from a couple of hundred yards away and followed Beth's oral directions which led him to the hidden narrow path that took him behind the screening curtain of water into a dim, damp cave.

He was mighty tired. He off-saddled the roan, spilled a cupful of grain Beth had given him on the ground in front of it and dumped his own meagre bedroll against the wall.

He figured he would sleep the clock around.

Wrong! The unfamiliar splashing and spluttering of the waterfall kept him awake, disturbing him hour after hour.

Zachariah Gunn was in a right old mood when enough daylight seeped in to convince him that it was well past sunrise. He had accumulated less than two hours' deep sleep.

At least he didn't have to go far to fill the coffee pot with water – just thrust out his hand at the cave entrance. Even that made him swear as the water splashed his clothes and left them sodden all down one side.

'Goddamn waterfall!' he said aloud for the twentieth time.

But with hot coffee and a few of Beth's biscuits – starting to get a little stale now – inside him, he mellowed and built himself a sliver-thin cigarette from the few tobacco flakes he had spread to dry on a rock. The smoke helped calm him and he eased past the edge of the waterfall, shielding the cigarette with curled fingers, until he found a rock to sit on where he could see, between two larger boulders, the broken country he had crossed. Gunn was so tired that he dozed off with only half his cigarette smoked. He awoke with a start, didn't know where he was, grabbed for the Spencer rifle he had laid beside him earlier.

And suddenly he was fully awake, senses tuned to his situation, heart hammering: his groping hand had failed to find the weapon.

He realized that it was behind him when someone cocked the hammer. Gunn hitched around as fast as he could, but he was in an awkward position, sitting down, and didn't get his pistol free of the holster before a harsh voice snapped:

'She sure picked a doozy when you turned up! Gonna look out for you, you told her.' The man spat. 'In a pig's eye! You couldn't look out for a church spire, 'less it hit you in the ass and the clock struck high noon.'

Gunn clambered up and glimpsed a man with wide shoulders and bristly yellow hair, who took a long step forward and rammed the rifle barrel into Gunn's midriff. Zack grunted and his legs buckled. Big teeth flashed in a broad stubbled face as the intruder swung the Spencer butt around in a short, jerky arc, aiming to crash the iron-clad butt against Gunn's head.

Gunn reacted by pure instinct, let his legs fold as he doubled over and the deadly butt whistled above his head, close enough to knock his hat off.

The attacker was startled, stumbled forward a step with his effort, and lifted the Spencer for another swipe. Gunn thrust with his boots against the rock and drove his head like a battering ram into the yellow-haired man's midriff.

The man grunted and staggered back, grunted again as the rough boulder surface raked his spine and drove air from his lungs. Dazed, he stumbled to one side, where Gunn was waiting, a mite breathless but in full fighting form. He weaved a little, for no reason: it just seemed to come as a natural precautionary movement, and then, dodging a clumsy blow, he stepped in as the other straightened painfully.

His fist cracked against the big square jaw and pain

surged across his knuckles and through his hand. It took him by surprise and delayed his follow-through. The square-jawed man bared his teeth, now showing a thin smear of blood, and a fist like a ham hock took Gunn under the ribs. He spun to one side, driven back by the force of the blow, stumbling. He put down a hand to keep from falling. The other man kicked it from under him and stomped on his back. Gunn was flattened against the rock which, naturally, had little give. His nose was bent and bleeding, his teeth cut the inside of his mouth. His chin was scraped raw. He rolled and slowly stood upright. He was halfway there when the attacker closed in a running charge that ended with a boot taking Gunn in the side and almost tearing his ribs loose.

The yellow-haired man bared his teeth, stepped back swiftly as his victim spread out on the rock, hands hanging briefly over the edge, a trace of blood showing through his unkempt hair.

The man lifted the rifle, spat on Zack's moaning form, then drew back his right boot and kicked out at Zack's nodding head. Gunn had enough sense to see it coming through the red haze smearing his vision. He dropped flat again, almost pressing his body into the rock. The boot heel skidded across the point of his shoulder, causing him to grunt, his body to jerk.

'Lousy goddam Reb!' the man raged as he stumbled, but quickly regained his balance. He lifted the rifle by the barrel in both hands, but something stopped him from swinging the weapon and smashing Gunn's brains out. Instead, he spat on his victim again. 'Lousy goddamn Reb!'

'You – already said – that. Damn Yankee.'

Sounds like the War's starting all over again, Gunn thought wryly, his head throbbing like a Sioux war drum. Breathing hard, he sat down on the rock. Opposite, the Yankee took a cheroot from his shirt pocket, lit it and blew smoke into Gunn's bleeding face.

'You an' me've got a powwow due, Reb. An' I need you able to savvy what I'm sayin'. I figure you don't, or *won't* do what I tell you. . . .' His big teeth showed again, half-clenched as he lifted the Spencer and recocked the hammer.

There was no reply, no reaction from the dazed Reb.

The yellow-haired man smoked, lowered the gun hammer, frowning. He walked across and nudged Zack Gunn roughly with a boot. 'Gerraway!' Gunn groaned. started to rise but halfway he sagged back and the big man drew back his boot again, this time aiming to get some more force into the kick.

Then there was a reaction from Mr Gunn.

His hands whipped out in a blur, locked around the scuffed riding-boot, gripped hard and heaved. Caught off balance, the yellow-haired man did an impromptu dance, staggering. By that time Gunn was on his feet, closing, with both fists swinging. One connected with the other's jaw, turning his head so violently that it slammed into the rock. Blood flowed down the rugged face, then Gunn's hands changed their grip to the corduroy shirt, took the weight as the man sagged.

Gunn eased him down, none too gently, against the rock and lightly slapped him across the bloody cheeks, back and forth.

'Wake up! C'mon, you Yankee son of a bitch! Let's see

57

how tough you are!'

But the man was still dazed; his head was lolling. Snorting now with impatience, having taken all the beating he aimed to, Gunn dragged the man along the precarious ledge to where the screening waterfall thundered over the hidden entrance. Grunting again, Gunn heaved the unconscious Yankee up and held him under the thundering water. It came with such force the man was almost torn from his grasp and he sucked in a sharp breath at the water's coldness.

In moments the yellow-haired man was writhing and gasping and choking, spitting, coughing, beginning to panic as he thought he was drowning.

He could have drowned easily, but Gunn yanked him away and pushed him back along the narrow track to where they had scuffled near the big boulders. He shoved him roughly and the man sprawled, rolled half on to his back, blinking and retching water.

Gunn leaned down and took the pistol from the sodden holster. It might or might not fire after that soaking, but he cocked the hammer anyway and thrust the muzzle between the other's eyes.

'You'd have to be Lobo, right?'

The yellow-haired man glared and Gunn moved the cold muzzle down to the bruised and bleeding cheek. He turned it slightly so that the blade foresight bit deep into the already bruised flesh.

'I didn't hear your answer.' Gunn pressed hard and the half-drowned man tried to turn his head, afraid that the sight was going to rip across his face.

'OK. I'm Lobo – McRae.'

'Self-appointed guardian of Beth Landis, right?'

This time Gunn increased the gunsight's pressure and McRae winced, nodded, his eyes dangerous but mighty leery of this wild-eyed, cold-voiced Johnny Reb who was one helluva lot tougher than the halfwit he had mistaken him for.

'I'd've married her if Landis hadn't swept her off her feet.'

'I doubt it. You might've offered – and she might've refused.'

'Like hell! I'd've died for her. Still will, if I have to!' He curled a split lip in a sneer. 'But I was just a sergeant and he was a captain and he had the money; enough to buy that small farm. If I coulda gotten hold of some land in time I'd've won her over.'

'All water down the creek now, anyway,' Gunn said, easing the pressure on the gunsight: there was a deep puckered ditch dug into Lobo's face where the metal blade had rested. 'One thing you were right about: we need to powwow. You can start by tellin' me what the hell you're doing here, and how you found this place.'

'That last bit's easy. I showed it to Beth long ago and – well, I'd been watchin' her place, saw you send Murray and his men on their way and then you rode out.'

'So you wanted to see her when she was on her own?'

'Just findin' out who the hell you are and what you were doin there.' He grinned with a half-sneer. 'Doesn't think much of you, is my guess. Asked me to come out and keep an eye on you.'

Then he suddenly hugged himself and his teeth

chattered. 'Judas priest! That water's freezin'. How about we go back to the cave and light a fire where we can both dry out?'

It made sense and Gunn nodded, jerking the pistol.

'Lead the way . . . mighty carefully.'

Surprisingly, Lobo was more cooperative, as if he had put Gunn to some kind of a test and Zack had apparently passed, or at least measured up in some way.

'I had ideas of courtin' her, way back,' Lobo started, obviously uncomfortable. He shook his head. 'Never had any real chance, specially after Captain Burt Lansing showed up.'

Gunn was smoking one of Lobo's cheroots now. He exhaled before speaking. 'Thought you were all for the good captain?'

Lobo shrugged. 'Well, he did save my neck when we were fightin' your lot. I might not have too many of them things they call scruples, but that was a debt I figured I just had to repay sometime.'

'And that time came – when?'

'Another damn battle – river-fight.'

'This Hellfire Bend Beth mentioned?'

Lobo frowned but nodded slowly. 'Yeah. It was a big one, as you likely know. We were outnumbered, our cannon carriage had busted so we couldn't use the gun, horses were down, some men ridin' double. A goddamn mess!' He was silent for a time, remembering.

He savagely rammed his cheroot butt against the rock and ground it to ashes. 'Landis knew we were goin' to lose but he had his orders: hold the crossin' at all costs.

Called me into his tent and said if anythin' happened to him, he wanted me to take care of Beth.'

Gunn let him have another long silence. 'I give him my word. Seemed like a nice easy chore. Huh! Never seen such an independent woman. Because the captain was listed only as 'missing' she never gave up hope he might still be alive.'

'Then I turned up with his jacket.'

Lobo's eyes narrowed. 'An' you dunno who the hell you are, she said!'

Obviously, Lobo didn't care to believe that.

'That's right. Far as I'm concerned the world began the day I woke up in a ditch with half a mountain pummelled flat by cannon fire all around me. Only name I knew was Burton Landis, because it was stitched into that jacket. Can recall takin' it off a dead man but whether *he* was Landis or not. . . .' He shrugged.

Lobo was watching him closely. 'Coulda been anyone, I guess. Someone else mighta done the same thing as you; saw the jacket on a dead man and took it.'

'Well, that's the way it is. Look, how much danger is Beth in? By me moving on, I mean. Murray struck me as the kinda *hombre* who'd call that harbouring a wanted man.'

'Damn right he will! That's what made me so mad – you leavin' her to face whatever he throws at her now.'

'Except you're still keeping your word to Landis.'

Lobo's big swollen jaw hardened. 'Bet your damn life on that! An' I'll throw you to Murray an' his wolves in the blink of an eye if I figure it's what it takes for him to leave Beth alone.'

Gunn nodded gently: it was about what he had expected.

'Where do we go from here?'

'You stay put. This is a good hidin' place. I'll go back, watch out for Beth. You see a chance to break for it, take it.'

Gunn smiled crookedly. 'Think I'd make it?'

'Not likely.'

'That's what I thought.'

Lobo stared levelly, then sighed. 'She's got a soft spot for you, for some reason. Likely because you stood up to Murray, who's given her a lot of damn trouble on behalf of the Reconstruction.'

'Why they picking on her? I mean, she's the widow of one of their heroes.'

Lobo hesitated. 'I ain't sure. Somethin' to do with the farm, mebbe. I get the feelin' Murray'd rather she wasn't runnin' it.'

'What's so important about the farm? Hell, it's rundown, land doesn't look like it'd grow a potato as big as an egg.'

'You'd know, huh?'

Gunn frowned. How did he know that about the land?

'Won't know nothin' 'less you tell me.'

'All I know is it's the only farm with undergound water, if that counts for anythin'. Landis blasted a deep well; you likely seen it. And that's it.' Lobo snapped those last words and Gunn thought right away that the man did know more but wasn't about to tell him.

'Listen,' Lobo resumed. 'I'll tell you how to get outta this country, or draw you a map, and then you're on your own. You see a chance, you take it. I mean it.'

Sure. Make a run for it, and if you do get out don't come back. Ever!

That was the way Lobo wanted it.

CHAPTER 7

'BRING ME THAT REB!'

Gunn knew Lobo would be watching him ride out in the direction he had suggested. He paused on a rise, took the crude map McRae had drawn him and spread it out on his thighs. While he appeared to study it – and he *did* scan the smeared lines of charcoal that Lobo had drawn – he looked at the surrounding country from under his hatbrim.

Still memorizing Beth's sketch map, he could pick pick out certain landmarks and also some others that Lobo had marked on his map. He soon traced his trail up to the waterfall hideout and then on to where he sat right now.

He nodded with a grim smile: he was riding slap-bang into country that Murray's troopers would be sure to be searching. And they would be travelling towards this

64

neck of the woods where he was even now. As if Lobo didn't know!

The hell he didn't! He'd deliberately directed Gunn into the path of Murray's search.

Right now there could be some officer's field glasses trained on him; or, worse, the sights of a rifle.

Still pretending to study the maps, he raked his gaze around, watching for movement. He spotted some birds fluttering over a pothole with some water in it. Another sat high on a tree branch, head turning this way and that – on watch? At ground level he saw a small disturbance that he figured could have been a snake or lizard sliding into cover.

The dust drifted across the slope in the mild breeze and his gaze was drawn naturally to it. But he wrenched his eyes upward, refusing to be mesmerized by the dancing dust devils. He glimpsed a patch of deep blue quickly cross a gap between two close-growing trees, followed by a pale, speckled flash of what could only be the rump of the rider's horse.

Without hesitation he crammed the map into his pocket, already using his other hand to pull the roan's head around and urged it down slope.

Anyone searching for him would expect him to go *up*, so he could keep his eye on the country below. But he didn't care if they were above him right now, because they were too far away to intercept him. He knew where he wanted to go, hoping like hell that Lobo had marked the area correctly. The roan's rump went down as its hind legs bent and the hoofs dug in. Dust would rise and they would have his position in minutes, but he kept the horse going down . . . down. Then, abruptly, he angled across the slope, just as three rifle shots boomed and crackled through the hills.

He neither saw nor heard the bullets, but those were just the first hasty shots, fired as they spotted him. By now they'd be sighting in and he weaved the horse roughly, having no choice, bringing snorting whinnies of protest from it. But it was still a compliant animal, answered the pressure on the reins and from his knees, the touch of his heels.

It weaved a couple of more times, then he jammed his heels in hard, yelled into its right ear and wrenched upward on the reins as they reached a ledge partly screened by a flat, jutting rock above.

Then they were airborne, the horse reacting instinctively. As they dropped vertically and forward on the slope, there was a volley of rifle fire and the thud of a couple of pistols.

Murray must have a good-sized band of hunters, with all that firepower: troopers and pistol-packing officers.

He heard the bullets this time, rattling through brush, one clipping a sapling, flicking a handful of bark and splinters. The slug snarled away in ricochet. Two more whipped air overhead and were lost in the brush below, where the roan plunged with a whinny and a convulsion that almost unseated Gunn.

He used the reins mercilessly, cuffed the roan once on an ear and shouted. No doubt the animal was surprised and maybe its feelings were hurt, for up until now he had been a patient and considerate rider. But maybe it realized that now it was time to pay back those past kindnesses.

With contortions that had Gunn wriggling in the saddle, slipping his boots from the stirrups, then hurriedly replacing them, they plunged into really heavy brush. He hoped it was closing up behind them, even though his progress was bound to be noticeable from above, but any kind of cover was acceptable right now, however briefly.

He shielded his eyes as branches whipped across his face, scraped his neck, slapped at his torso. He felt for the Spencer in the hastily made rope sling. It was still attached to the saddle, but taking a battering. He steadied it by gripping the comb of the stock, not attempting to draw the weapon out of the sling's loop. Not yet! But the time would come and he tried to recall how much ammuntiion he had. Not much! Only one spare magazine tube, loaded: that meant seven shots, ready to replace the tube already in the rifle's butt when it was emptied. Maybe four left in that.

It would be time enough to worry about it when he was shooting back.

That time might not be long in coming.

For now he had to concentrate on crashing through this brush and, if Lobo's map was true, finding his way on to a trail that would lead him to a creek that wound into a deep canyon. There, Lobo had claimed, he would find plenty of caves to hide in.

But Gunn reckoned Lobo hadn't really figured on him getting that far . . . maybe not even *this* far, the son of a bitch!

He had been set up. He'd been aware of the risk, but what choice did he have in country that was as strange to him as the streets of Washington?

The roan suddenly changed its movement into a side-ways action, jarring him in the saddle, as it crashed through a line of brush. And there it was!

There was the stony, cluttered trail leading out of this arroyo, which in turn led to the flat banks of a creek which disappeared between the rugged, rising walls of a knife-blade canyon. He set the horse towards the entrance, hearing yells behind and above as someone spotted him.

Rifles thudded and echoed as he ran the sure-footed roan across the narrow creek and between the high walls where deep shadows helped hide him from marksmen above.

The canyon, little more than a defile through this low mountain, was so narrow that sunlight didn't reach the floor. An instant later he realized this was little advantage: he had nowhere to go *but* along the trail that took random turns on its way to an exit that he was unable to see.

But the men above could!

Then there was a heavy volley. He winced and jerked in the saddle as lead whipped and buzzed around him. The roan shrilled and plunged wildly, momentarily jamming his left leg against the wall. He yelled a curse and lay quickly along the mount's back. More slugs hammered against the walls and one amongst the lethal swarm laid a burning gash on the roan's left shoulder. It whinnied and plunged, rump swinging wildly into the wall. In his half-prone position with his left leg held stiffly, boot free of the stirrup, he was suddenly swept out of the saddle by a low-hanging branch almost exactly at his head's height.

The world somersaulted and tilted, then jarred violently as he hit the ground, bouncing off the wall itself. Red flashes burst behind his eyes. The horse ran on, frightened and no doubt hurting.

As some sense dribbled back into his semiconsciousness he realized he'd dropped the Spencer. Rolling, he reached out blindly, sweeping his arms across the stony ground, and felt the butt of the weapon. As his hand closed over it, a bullet struck sparks from the hammer and the Spencer jumped wildly as the impact caused the round in the chamber to discharge.

The gun leapt out of reach. Then the narrow space was crammed with riders who threatened him with smoking rifles.

'Don't kill him!' a voice boomed from a narrow ledge several feet above. 'Bring that damn Reb to me!'

Gunn recognized Murray's voice. Then Lieutenant Killen walked his dusty mount forward, covering him with his Remington pistol.

'You heard the major, Reb. You wanna walk in, or crawl with a slug through your belly?'

Short of breath, bleeding from scratches and grazes, limping as his injured leg took his weight, Gunn lifted his hands out to his side, raising them slowly.

'Reckon I'll walk.'

'While you can,' Killen growled, nudging his mount forward, freeing a boot from the stirrup and kicking at Gunn's head.

The Reb just managed to jerk aside but the heavy boot

took him in the shoulder and sent him staggering. It felt as if his collarbone was broken and he grabbed at it even while he fought to stay upright.

'Let's move!' the lieutenant snapped. 'Major Murray wants to get outta this lousy canyon. We been here too damn long as it is.'

Gunn looked up, blinking a little blood out of his left eye. 'Lobo set me up, didn't he?'

Killen smiled crookedly. 'You fell for it, whoever did it.'

Gunn nodded, bitter thoughts swirling through his mind. The fact that he'd had no choice but to follow Lobo's directions wasn't much comfort.

'I said bring that damn Reb to me!' Major Murray's voice boomed impatiently. 'That would mean right now!'

'Comin', Major! Our poor little Reb is feelin' a mite poorly at this moment.'

'He'll hardly notice when he finds out what's going to happen to him!'

Under Reconstruction law it was perfectly legal what they did to Mr Gunn.

They even gave him a chance to tell his version.

This didn't mean that they took more than passing notice of what he said, but it would look good on their records: *Rebel prisoner encouraged to tell his version of events in his own words. . . .*' What could be fairer?

They tried not to mention too many times that he was an ex-soldier of the Confederate Army; no use getting too many backs up in the district. Truth was, the enforcers of Reconstruction were having more than enough trouble with local Rebs who didn't take kindly to being pushed around.

Yet they had to satisfy everyone that Gunn had been given every chance to explain his behaviour, even, when you got right down to it, why he had broken Reconstruction law. Penalties were harsh, the 'investigation' perfunctory but made to look thorough enough on paper.

A 'search' was arranged for the original owner of the roan horse: the gambler who had lost the game where the horse had been originally wagered. He was never found, which was a blow to Gunn, because he had no one to back his side of the story now.

There was no real court. What took place was more a hearing before Judge Ethan Holman, an ex-general, appointed by the Reconstruction Commission to handle such cases. He was a clear-eyed sixty-year-old with a pointed beard, and a long line of medals from memorable victories pulling at his neatly pressed blue tunic. It was boasted that there was never a need for a jury when Judge Holman was in charge.

But Holman listened attentively as Gunn told his version of how he came to claim ownership of the roan with the white rump. He even made a note or two when the accused reached the point where he had seen the horse tied to a hitchrail outside a Boulder saloon.

'And you decided to steal it there and then?'

'No, sir. I decided that as it was my horse, I had every right to take it.'

The judge's eyes glittered. He stared and with a scowl wrote something in his notebook with such ferocity that he broke the pen nib. He irritably waved away the attentive clerk who handed him a replacement.

'In the alley,' Holman said gratingly, 'where you found Josh Creedy had just relieved his bladder, you kicked him in the head?'

'I was aiming to kick his pistol out of his hand, Judge. I wasn't armed.'

'Nor should you have been! But it is the action I am interested in: you *kicked* him in the head.' As Gunn tiredly tried to explain again the judge roared him down, and shook a finger at him. 'Don't you come your smart-ass Rebel yelling at me, mister! You kicked a man in the head and he was later found in the same area, kicked to death! Have you enough brains to see what I'm getting at?'

'Unfortunately, Judge, I do!' Gunn gritted. 'But I did not kick Josh Creedy more than once and my horse did not stomp on him as I rode off – in case you might've figured that as an alternative.'

An armed soldier nearby the table where Gunn stood received an urgent signal from Major Murray and the man slammed his rifle butt brutally into Gunn's midriff. He raised the weapon again as Gunn doubled forward over the table but Killen gestured for him to desist. The lieutenant looked at Gunn's red, blotched face as he fought for breath, twisting fingers in the Reb's hair.

'He's a mite dazed, Judge, but I reckon he could savvy your findings – if you've a mind to make 'em.'

Holman was obviously outraged. He stood up, gathering his papers as he said, ponderously, 'Zachariah Gunn, you are charged with the murder of one Joshua Creedy on. . . .' He paused and glared at his helper who was frantically looking through the papers for the exact date. 'Never mind, dammit! About three or four weeks ago is near enough. The point is, I find you guilty and the penalty is death by hanging. I herewith pronounce that such penalty shall be carried out with all expedition.'

He lifted his papers into his arms, glaring around at his audience: all Union Army officers and men. No civilians had been admitted to the hearing.

'Now, I fully intend to be on the train leaving for Denver at sundown and will not tolerate any delays. Major Murray, you will set the procedure in motion immediately if you please.'

The word soon spread: there was going to a hanging, the victim a Johnny Reb. This news caused some excitement: the town hadn't stretched a Reb's neck in a coon's age.

There had been many hangings right after the war in Climax and the resulting 'permanent' gallows always attracted a large crowd in festive mood. Legitimate hard liquor and not-so-legal moonshine soon turned a picnic-style gathering into a wild, raucous wingding that had been known on at least one occasion to get out of hand enough actually to delay the execution by over an hour. By that time, the victim was so drunk he didn't even know – or care, probably – what was happening to him. Some said he dropped through the trap still singing a chorus of 'Buffalo Gals'.

Yes! A hanging day was something to look forward to in Climax, Colorado. Everyone was guaranteed a good time.

Even, on occasion, the poor devil standing on the trap with the noose knotted around his neck, if you believed that 'Buffalo Gals' eyewash.

CHAPTER 8

NOT FOR THE HANGMAN

Lobo McRae had been keeping well clear of Beth Landis since Gunn's capture. Twice she had ridden up to his smallholding and once she was sure he was there, or close by, hiding in the brush and timber.

But he did not show himself and, frustrated, angry, she walked her horse around his yard, calling:

'I know you deliberately set Zack Gunn on to a trail that would take him into the search area, Lobo! You're a despicable traitorous fool and I warn you, don't come on to my land, or I'll shoot you on sight!'

She waited, hoping the threat would bring him into the open, but there was no sign of him.

Disgusted, she rode back to her farm and made coffee. Sitting at the table, she was surprised to see how badly her hand was shaking as she lifted the cup to her mouth.

My God! They're going to kill him! He'll be dead by sundown tomorrow. . . .

She seldom swore but she did now, surprising herself at the intensity of her words. It wasn't fair. It had happened before, too often, this quick, no-appeal 'trial' under Judge Holman. There were lots of folk, both Reb and Yankee, who were not happy with the harsh Reconstruction Administration and its methods; many of the officers who enforced the rules used them to settle old scores from before the war. It made no difference whether the victim was Northerner or Southerner. The Reconstruction Commission, of course, turned a blind eye to such doings.

Wise folk kept any thoughts along those lines to themselves; the Commission had eyes and ears everywhere. Land was land, whether it was 'legally' stolen from Southerner or Yankee. There were a surprising number of folk who called themselves 'Yankee' yet who still found themselves victims of the Reconstruction's desires. *Land was land, taxes were taxes.*

She knew Major Murray had been instructed to take over gradually, imposing tight 'laws', showing the world there was no favouritism here; if a man transgressed the new rulings, he paid for it, no matter his background. Of course, Yankees usually paid less of everything than out-and-out Rebs.

It was only the fact that Beth was the still unofficial widow of a Union war hero that had prevented a straight-out land grab in her case. Beth was popular, as had been Burton Landis, decorated war hero; even the Reconstruction had to tread carefully at times, but she would eventually lose the farm to Murray and his administration, she knew.

She stiffened, set down the coffee cup carefully, as she heard a horse quietly entering her yard. She grabbed the loaded single-barrel Greener shotgun and went to the ailing front door. She was surprised to see Lobo dismounting and looking mighty wary as she lifted the shotgun into line.

'Stay right there. Didn't you hear me up at your place? I said I'd shoot you on sight if you came here.'

He lifted his hands shoulder-high, swiftly. 'Hey, easy, Beth! OK, I heard, but you got it wrong. I never set up Gunn.'

'I'm in no mood for a string of your lies, Lobo.' She settled the gun butt more comfortably against her hip in her corduroy trousers and Lobo paled. 'The point is, your bungling has gotten Zack Gunn killed! Or as good as.'

'Hold up! Judas, gimme a chance to explain!' More quietly, he added, 'An' it might pay you not to push that story about Gunn bein' your brother, right now, Beth. You savvy what I mean?'

'We were discussing how you sent Gunn into the arms of Lieutenant Killen's search party!'

When he didn't answer, she merely waited, hammer spur under her thumb, finger curled around the trigger. Lobo licked his thick lips. 'Look, I drew him a sort of map at the waterfall cave. I had to use a lump of charcoal, and it smeared. I figure that was where he went wrong: couldn't read my directions clearly and took that trail through the defile where Killen jumped him after

I'd told him *not* to take it.'

'You're stretching a long bow, Lobo!' she snapped.

'No! It's true. I been thinkin' on it and it's the only way it coulda happened.' His voice became more wheedling. 'Hell, Beth, you know I look out for you, help you any way I can – or that you'll let me. I give my word to the cap'n on that and I swear I'll do it. I don't like that Reb, I admit, but you wanted him to get clear so I – I tried to show him a way out. Things just went wrong, is all.'

'About as wrong as they could! Zack Gunn is going to hang tomorrow!'

He shuffled his big feet uncomfortably. 'Yeah, well. Look, I'm bein' honest now, it don't matter spit to me whether he swings or not. Aw, OK, OK! I'd prefer he swings! All right? But there's nothin' can be done now. It's too late.'

Her eyes narrowed and she changed her grip slightly on the Greener: held it more firmly, as if she was getting ready to fire. Lobo licked his lips and his tongue rasped across them, they were so dry.

'Not as long as he's breathing. All it needs is for someone to get him out of that jail.'

Lobo's square jaw dropped. 'You're plumb loco. No one can get near that jailhouse. They got seven guards inside, all armed to the teeth, and mean as rattlesnakes.'

Beth stared, then nodded slowly. 'Yes – inside. But none outside.'

'What?' His eyes actually bulged and then he gave a derisive laugh. 'Woman, you – are – plumb – crazy! That jail was built before the war to hold the men they cap-tured in the Badman's Territory – killers every one. No one escaped. They couldn't! The damn walls are granite, nearly two feet thick!'

Her gaze held steady to his face until he began to squirm uneasily, shaking his head. 'Crazy!' he murmured.

'You know Burton made that well out there in my yard? He had to use dynamite in places. There's some left over in the barn. You once boasted that you were part of a demolition team that blew down an entire mountain.'

'Judas priest! Hell, woman, you're worse'n crazy! You're totally in-sane! Use enough dynamite to blast that wall and you'll kill whoever's on the other side, blow 'em to hell'n'gone.' He shook his head rapidly. 'No. Get used to the idea, Beth. There's no way to bust Gunn loose from that jail. Only way he's gonna leave this town is in a coffin.'

'You should never have come to Colorado, Gunn, or whatever your real name is.'

Major Murray stood outside the heavy bars of the cell door, seeing Gunn sitting uncomfortably on the edge of the narrow bunk, which had no bedclothes whatever on it. The cell was dim, too, as there were no windows. Now the Yankee pressed his face closer, felt the cold iron against his high-boned cheeks. 'You must have a death wish.'

'No more'n anyone else,' Gunn replied quietly. 'I came here trying to find out who I am.'

Murray smiled crookedly. 'Aren't you Beth Landis's long-lost brother?' he said slyly.

'Leave her out of this. She's got nothing to do with it.'

'I agree. But she's buying in. Makes me wonder why.'

Gunn stared coldly. 'Well, it won't matter after sundown tomorrow.'

'Mmmmm. I like to tie neat knots around a chore when it's finished, not leave ends trailing.'

'You'll manage to live with it.'

Murray chuckled. 'That I will!' He gestured to the bare bunk. 'I can get you a blanket and a pillow, if you want to take a nap.'

'Reckon I'll get all the sleep I need soon enough. Just go away, Murray. You turn my stomach.'

The major's eyes hardened. 'And here I was going to offer you a last meal of your choice!' He ran the short, leather-covered cane he held along the bars, making them ring. 'Reckon you can die hungry, Reb!' He started to turn away, then swung back. 'Just so long as you *die*!'

'See you in hell, Major.'

Gunn watched Murray walk down the short passage. The armed guard there opened the door for him, then closed it after he'd walked through.

'You should watch your mouth, Reb. You coulda had yourself some comfort before they drop you through that trapdoor.' The guard looked tough and gruff, but there was a touch of real concern at Gunn's stubbornness: he just didn't savvy it.

Gunn said nothing, stretched out on the uncomfortable bare boards of the bunk, locking his hands behind his head and staring up at the ceiling.

Damn! But he would've liked to find out who the hell

he really was before he took that fatal step on to the gallows.

He closed his eyes on that sombre thought but he knew there was little chance of sleep this night.

The town was full of drunken, yelling men accompanied by the occasional sound of breaking glass, and even a few gunshots.

The celebrations for Gallows Day were already under way: literally with a bang!

Lobo McRae was still at Beth's place when they heard a buckboard pull into the yard.

She had taken pity on Lobo and at his repeated requests had cooked him some supper. She had little appetite herself but in the back of her mind was the possibility that she might need to play on Lobo's conscience and his promise to her husband that he would look after her. *That*, she had decided, might well be interpreted as meaning he would do as she wished, under certain circumstances.

There was no one else to turn to, so if she really wanted to try to break Gunn out of jail, Lobo had to be the one to call on for help. . . .

Now, as the buckboard clattered to a stop outside, Lobo slurped down the last of the gravy from the plate of stew she had cooked for him, wiped the back of a hand quickly across his mouth and stood up, reaching for his six-gun.

Beth had grabbed her Greener and swung it swiftly to the permanently ajar front door as a man appeared there.

It was Haviland, the roly-poly Climax storekeeper, sweating and breathing hard as he wiped his reddened face.

Before she could speak, he blurted: 'Sorry to bust in like this, Beth! On my way to my son's place up-valley.' He gestured vaguely. 'Wife's not too well and I want to get her out of town. She's really scared.'

'Scared?' Beth echoed, trying to see past Haviland's shoulder and catching a brief glimpse of the woman huddling on the buckboard's seat.

'Town's gone crazy! First Reb to be hung for nigh on six months. Creedy and Devlin cut loose and have stirred things up because it was Creedy's brother that Gunn was s'posed to've killed for that horse. It's well out of hand. I've lost my street-front window again and one awning post'll have to be replaced. Lewis's barber shop was set on fire and half-burned. The livery. . . .' He shook his head again. 'They're even up on the roof of the jail, tearin' up shingles and threatening to drop snakes into Gunn's cell. It's just plain chaos and the Administration is sitting back and letting it happen.'

'Gotta allow the folk they're hittin' with new taxes and so on a little entertainment,' Lobo commented. Beth arched her eyebrows at his astuteness. 'Kickin' up hell, are they?'

Haviland nodded several times. 'I'm staying out of town until after the hanging. Lord knows how much of my store'll be there when I get back. Beth, have you any of that stomach balm you make up for the ladies who suffer with morning sickness? I don't mean to imply my wife is – well – you know. It's just her nerves, I think, and if you could sell me a bottle to see us on our way to Jethro's place. . . .'

'I still have a couple of bottles, Mr Haviland. I'll get you one. Never mind any payment.'

The storekeeper and his moaning wife pulled out of the yard ten minutes later. Lobo lit the cigarette he had rolled, and as he flicked away the vesta commented: 'You ask me, Haviland himself'll drink half that muck you gave him. *He*'s the one wants to stay clear of town. His belly's weaker than his wife's, and a whole damn lot bigger!'

She didn't seem to hear him. She started to lift down her hat from a wallpeg and a bridle from alongside.

'Where the hell you goin'?'

Her eyes were bright as she lifted the shotgun and started for the door. 'To town, of course. . . .' She paused as he frowned.

'You just heard Haviland say it's like a madhouse in there,' hobo said. 'A drunken mob on the loose; no place for you.'

She smiled. 'Yes! A wild night indeed! And people cavorting up on the roof of the jailhouse!'

His mouth dropped open so swiftly that the freshly lit cigarette fell to the earthen floor in a shower of sparks. 'Hell almighty!' he breathed. 'You ain't serious!'

'Are you coming?' she demanded impatiently.

CHAPTER 9

WIDE OPEN TOWN

Major Murray was discreetly absent from the streets of Climax. He found he had business out of town – *well* out of town – at a dairy farm near the foot of the second mountain range.

He claimed that the men in his charge were not getting enough of the right kind of food; he wanted to arrange a contract with the dairy farmer, Miles Huckabee, who had been ailing for a long time, mostly bedridden, and couldn't be expected to call on the major at his headquarters.

'Something like this will help perk him up,' the major told Huckabee's much younger wife, winking the eye on the side away from the sallow, droopy-eyed, middle-aged man in the big rumpled bed.

'D'you hear that, Miles, dear?' young Gretchen Huckabee asked, sounding enthusiastic. 'Just what we need! A solid contract with the major's administration!

Oh, I'm sure you'll feel much better once it's arranged.'

'Er . . . yes, well, Gretchen,' said the major. 'Perhaps you and I could go through to the parlour and work out some terms acceptable to both of us. Later I'll bring it in for Miles to sign. Or, if he's agreeable, you can sign on his behalf.'

'That's a good idea!' Gretchen moved to the bed and began to arrange the pillows and bedclothes around her sick husband who watched her but didn't speak. 'You get some sleep, Miles, while the major explains to me just what he has in mind.'

If Miles Huckabee hadn't been feeling so poorly, just one look at Murray's face would have told him exactly what the major had in mind.

Lieutenant Killen knew what Murray was really doing out at the Huckabee place and he cursed the major good.

'Runs out, leaves me with the town bustin' its britches, half our men joinin' the shindig, and he won't turn up till hangin' time. Then he'll blast the socks off me for lettin' things get so goddam wild. I been there, done that!'

He ranted and raved, countermanded orders and eventually admitted the mob were by now too drunk to obey any of his instructions, anyway. Sweating, stomach knotted tighter than a cinch-strap, he finally said to hell with it.

Gunn couldn't be busted out of the jail anyway, because Killen had the only key, so let the mob run loose. They'd all have hangovers by tomorrow and that'd make it easier to bully 'em when gallows time arrived.

Meantime, there was that golden-skinned new whore at Pecos Hattie's. One of his troopers, trying to ingratiate himself with Killen, had given a graphic description of her talents.

'She's half-Portagee, Lieutenant, an' half-Mex. Man, talk about a brushfire in skirts. . . .'

So Killen hurried to Hattie's to see for himself. He was well on the way to agreeing with his trooper about the new girl's talents when there was a commotion in the passage outside the room where he and the Portagee temptress were entwined.

'Fire! Fire! Judas, c'mon, fellers! Get out here an' lend a hand before the whole damn place burns down!'

Killen swore. Doors were slamming and men were running down passageways, yelling or cursing or both. He hitched up his trousers, looked regretfully down at the naked girl, and added an obscene curse about his luck – or lack of it.

'Just ain't my goddamn night!' he roared wrenching open the door and coughing as he breathed in a thick pall of choking smoke. Tears streaming, he joined the mad throng of running men and screaming whores as the smoke and flames swirled through the passage. A bucket brigade had already started, but booze made it uncoordinated, and so ineffective. Sighing, Killen waded in, shouting orders above the din, trying to organize the panic. *Goddammit!* He'd be here for hours!

Beth Landis crouched in the darkness behind the jail-house, where there was a lot of yelling, the sounds of a couple of brawls, and some really bad off-key singing of well-worn trail ditties. She turned swiftly as Lobo came

86

hurrying up, panting as he dropped down beside her, smelling strongly of coal oil.

He gulped. 'Half the men in town're fightin' the whorehouse fire. Other half are drunk, an' mostly in there!' He gestured to the jail with a thumb. 'Hey! You got a mean streak, Beth, you know, tellin' me to start a fire behind the whorehouse!'

'Makes sense, doesn't it? Men would rather try to save Pecos Hattie's, and maybe get a glimpse of some naked flesh, than kick up a fuss at the jail where they know they can't even get at a man due to hang anyway.'

Lobo chuckled. 'You got an angel's face, Beth, but you know a lot more'n folk figure!'

There was a sudden wild yell from the sloping roof of the jailhouse, a different sound from the drunken cater-wauling that had been filling the night until now. It was followed by a splintering crash, and a man's frantic yell that cut off abruptly.

'The hell was that?' Lobo breathed, sliding his gun into his hand.

'I think that drunk up on the roof with the rattlensake must've fallen through the shingles.'

'Hell! I wouldn't want to be in that cell with a rattler all riled up an' on the loose.'

Beth grabbed his arm and pointed. There was just enough light to see what looked like a length of heavy rope fall from the roof to the ground several feet from where they crouched. She tugged hard as she felt Lobo instinctively start to jump up. 'Stay still. It'll go away!'

'Long as it ain't in this direction.'

She was sure she could see the whites of Lobo's

widened eyes. 'C'mon! We have to get up on that roof now that there's no one else up there.'

'Now look, Beth—'

'Oh, shut up, Lobo! Help me on to that upturned barrel and bring the rope. There's no other way!'

She was already climbing on to the big keg. He sighed, stood up and, careful where he walked, slung the coil of knotted rope around his left arm. He helped her find a footing on the barrel, then she reached for the edge of the sloping roof, the long poncho she wore making rasping sounds.

There was still a lot of racket coming from inside the jailhouse itself and, cautiously, lying full length on the loosened shingles, Beth pulled herself to the edge of the hole and looked down into the cell.

Light from the passage down below shone into the cell, although there were plenty of deep shadows, too. Men with bottles in their hands – or up to their mouths – crowded against the bars. She could just make out Gunn in the cell bending over a sprawled form she knew must be the drunk who had tried to drop the snake in.

'Ah, shoot!' a slurred voice said through the bars. 'Hooley's gone'n' fell in an' lost the damn snake.'

'Think he's broke a leg,' Gunn informed them, examining the unconscious man. 'Or his neck.'

'Never could hold his likker, Ol' Hooley. Shoulda let me do the job,' a swaying, bleary-eyed townsman said.

'You wanta take over?' someone asked quickly.

'What I want is 'nother bottle of thish moonshine. Where's Sting Carey? *Sthing*! Gimme another jug, huh? I'll fix you up come payday.'

There began an argument about payment and jostling men moved away from the cell door, as a uniformed guard poked his head around the passage and shouted,

'Hey! The hell're you fellers doin' wastin' your time here? Man, there's whores runnin' everywheres down at Hattie's with no clothes on! Bare-butt nekked, I swear!'

He was almost trampled in the rushing exodus as men struggled and fought to get down the narrow passage to the street door. In seconds, there was only empty space outside Gunn's cell.

Beth saw Gunn lift the injured Hooley on to the bunk, She called softly, her voice startling Gunn.

'Lay him on the bunk with your hat over his face, Zack. That mob're so drunk they won't even remember Ben Hooley falling in. Now get ready to climb this knotted rope. With any luck that crazy mob won't even realize you've gone when they get back.'

Gunn blinked, staring up at her silhouette against the stars, then he dodged as the heavy knotted rope fell down in front of his face, swaying back and forth.

'Don't waste time!' Beth hissed. 'The knots are only two feet apart. Start climbing and we'll get out of town before anyone knows it. Come on, Zack! Start climbing!'

He wrapped his hands around a knot as high as he could reach, pulled himself up enough to let the rope twist about his legs, then clamped another of the big knots between his boots. He grunted as he heaved and rose almost his full body length before he repeated the process. Beth guided the rope past the splintered edge. She could hear Lobo's grunts from down in the alley as he took the strain on the other end, the rope looped under his buttocks, hands burning against the fibres as he backed away slowly, keeping it taut. Sweat streamed down his face as he gritted his teeth.

In no time at all Gunn was being pulled through the roof-hole by Beth. They clambered down to where Lobo waited.

The town was lit by the flickering flames now eating into Pecos Hattie's Pleasure Parlour, a scene of utter chaos, backed by screams and breaking glass, and the mostly ineffective sloshing of water from buckets dipped in the nearby creek, then passed hand-to-hand along a wavering line of stumbling drunks, much being spilt in the process.

Standing aside from the main crowd were two townswomen, hard workers in the Episcopalian Church at the north edge of town. They clasped their hands in prayer, requesting the Good Lord to allow the flames to consume this den of sin.

Gunn and his rescuers were about to step towards the waiting getaway mounts when a cold voice, the edges slightly slurred by drink, asked harshly:

'What the hell's goin' on here?'

They turned swiftly, and glimpsed a corporal's stripes on a blue sleeve; a pistol in a big, gnarled fist was covering them. Gunn still held the rope, had almost finished coiling it after it had done its job. Without hesitation, he swung it, in an arc. The solid, heavy knots hit the soldier across the head like a kick from a mule. The man was knocked completely off his feet and, apart from a startled grunt, didn't make a sound as he lay still.

Gunn leapt forward and unbuckled the gunbelt with

its pouch of spare percussion caps, powder flask and wads. As he buckled the rig about his own waist he knew by the small size of the gun's butt that it was a Remington Army issue of 1858, the butt being of one of that excellent weapon's few drawbacks. It had better mechanism and loading ease than the Colts of that era, but those undersize handgrips caused a deal of fumbling till a man got used to them.

'Hurry up,' cried Beth, her nervousness plain in her voice. 'Someone must have sent him down to check on the jail when those drunks abandoned it for the whorehouse fire. They may come looking for him!'

They hit leather fast, wheeled the mounts swiftly, the hoofs clattering unavoidably. But no one noticed the three dark riders clearing the opposite side of town.

Lobo led the way.

He guided them along a boulder-strewn trail that dropped downslope into a creek. Here he put his mount into the shallow water; Beth and Gunn followed. Gunn was riding a strange horse, one of Lobo's ranch animals. He figured he would never see the roan with the white patch again and felt a sense of loss. But he had to wrench sharply on the reins and swing the head of the big dun under him, ducking as a low-sweeping bough of a tree leaning out from the creek bank whipped across his face.

'Keep your mind on what we're doin', goddammit!' Lobo swore. 'We got a ways to go upstream yet.'

It seemed to Gunn they rode for hours, but it was barely half an hour: the glow from the fire in the town was still plainly visible when they looked back.

'Likely have a massive manhunt for the man who burned down the local whorehouse,' Gunn commented.

'Yeah!' Lobo said bitterly. 'An' to think I stuck my neck out for you!'

'Aw, I'd do the same for you, Lobo, you know that,' Gunn said, starting to relax some now; it had been a strain sitting alone in his cell with nothing to think about during the last few hours before the hangman dropped him through the gallows trap. But he would have liked to know who he really was before that happened.

Such thoughts had only increased the pressure: he'd begun to worry they might even lynch him on the spot. Except that they weren't able to get into the cell.

'Jokin' aside,' he said gruffly, 'I'm almighty obliged to you both.'

'You'll square with me some way,' Lobo told him. 'I'll figure somethin' out.' He glanced at Beth, adding, 'An' I didn't do it for you, Gunn.'

'Still obliged.'

Beth said quietly, 'I think we should concentrate on getting clear. Lobo, when do we leave this creek?'

'Comin' right up.' McRae let his horse drop back beside the girl and Gunn. 'What you gonna do with him?'

Beth snapped her head up; there was enough moonlight to see her frown of puzzlement.

Lobo made an exasperated sound. 'Dammit, Beth! He can't stay with you. An' he sure damn well ain't gonna stay with me.'

She looked soberly at Gunn. 'That is something of a problem, Zack. Murray will search my place very quickly.'

'I'll go back to the waterfall cave. Murray doesn't know about that, does he?'

'Mebbe not, but some local might. He could tell Murray, tryin' to keep in his good books.'

'Well, I guess I'll find some place, or just ride clear of this neck of the woods altogether.'

'It's not going to be that easy, Zack! The Reconstruction convicted you of the murder of one of their own. Things are very touchy right now, with 'most everyone hating them because of the heavy taxes and land confiscation. Murray can't afford to fail on this manhunt. He'll order his men to bring you in at any cost.'

'Dead or alive,' Lobo added with a certain relish. 'Preferably dead, I'd reckon.'

They rode in silence for a time, getting their mounts out of the creek and on to ground hard enough not to take an easily discernible track. Silently, Lobo led the way over a rise and through a long, twisting arroyo that brought them out at the river.

'We swim the hosses across and go out t'other side, leavin' some tracks pointin' upstream. But swing back pronto into the river, let the current carry us downstream.'

'That's a dangerous move, Lobo!' Beth said sharply. 'The current's very strong here and this part of the river runs across Bryce McCall's land.'

'No choice. We'll clear it soon as we can. When we get far enough south of the Half-Moon line, you'll be able to cut back to your place, Beth.'

'And you and Zack?'

'Well, I know where I'm goin'. It's up to Gunn where he wants to go.'

'Lobo, that's not fair! Zack doesn't know this country! If he's seen trespassing on Half-Moon they're just as likely to shoot him on sight!'

'Now wouldn't that be a shame.'

Gunn glared at Lobo, but he knew the man couldn't see his face clearly, and that it wouldn't make any differ-ence if he could. As Beth started to speak, he said,

'You two've done enough. I'll take my chances. No! That's an end to it, Beth. Can't let you stick your neck out any more. I'll make sure I steer clear of Half-Moon. Even if I'm caught they'll never know who helped me.'

'Just hope that damn soldier you hit didn't recognize Beth,' growled Lobo.

But it wasn't likely. It had all happened very quickly and she had been wearing a neck-to-toe man's slicker anyway, as some form of disguise.

They both heard Beth suck in a sharp breath.

'Not likely he saw you as anything but another man in the dark, Beth,' Gunn said quietly, trying to reassure her.

'Anyways, our main problem right now is where to dump this sonuver,' growled Lobo. 'I don't want to be anywhere near when they catch up with him. I got no hankerin' to step into a stray bullet.'

Suddenly Beth put up a hand, stopping the others.

'Wait! There's a chance I . . . yes! Yes, I know where you can hide – and Murray or Killen won't even think of looking there!'

Both men waited tensely for her to explain, Gunn's heart beating rapidly, his right hand tightening around the smooth cedar butt of the newly acquired Remington pistol.

Her next few words would determine his future.

CHAPTER 10

HIDEOUT

The buildings were in darkness: house, barn, stables, and only the starlight threw vague shadows. A couple of horses stomped and neighed in the corrals.

Then a dog's bark shattered the quiet. It was more of a yap than a full-throated bark, but it caused the three riders making their way into the ranch yard to rein up fast.

Lobo McRae unsheathed his rifle and Gunn started to lift the Remington from the leather. Mentally, he made a note to cut the flap from the Army-issue pouch as soon as he could, so that the gun would come free more smoothly and quickly.

Beth Landis merely tensed, looking around her for the dog. It was tethered to one of the corral posts and seemed to be facing away from the trio. It began to bark in earnest and Lobo stood in the stirrups, levering a cartridge into the rifle's breech. There was a scuffling sound

96

near the barn.

'Mebbe a coyote prowlin', looking for something to eat,' he said in a low voice, still straining to see.

'Or,' said a voice from the deep shadow on the barns. It was accompanied by the swift clash of metal as a rifle lever worked, 'Mebbe he's doin' his job and lettin' us know we got us three prowlers, who make damn fine targets agin the stars! Nope! Don't lift that rifle 'less you're ready to die, feller!'

Lobo froze. Beth's slicker rustled and Gunn's Remington stopped just clear of the holster lip.

'Go ahead, mister. Draw if you want. I can nail all three of you easy, if I put my mind to it.'

They were caught and they knew it. They did as they were told when the voice ordered them to sheathe their weapons and sit with hands folded on the saddle horns.

'Shut up, Pud!' the unseen gunman yelled at the dog now in full barking mode, but there was a touch of affection in the command and the dog settled down to a series of whimpers. 'Hear that wheeze? Overweight. Greedy sonuver never stops eatin'. Why we call him 'Pudden'. But if I let him loose and tell him to, he'll take your leg off, so just set real still.'

They each gave a small start as his last words were followed by a series of piercing whistles, which the guard made by manipulating his tongue, lips and teeth.

Within seconds there were sounds of men moving about the bunkhouse and a door at the main house opened part-way. A shotgun barrel protruded, reflecting some of the starlight.

'We got us visitors, Nate?' a voice drawled. 'I mean, I ain't really dressed for . . . receivin', you know?'

Nate chuckled. 'Three, Bryce. An' I think one's a woman tryin' to pass for a man by wearin' a long slicker.'

'Well, now, that sounds interestin'. How about you three dismount, slow'n' easy-like, startin' with the lady. If you ain't sure about doin' it, just take a leetle look around and you'll find at least half a dozen guns trained on you.'

'You're mighty edgy, Bryce,' called Lobo as he started to dismount carefully. His rifle was back in the saddle scabbard by now.

'I know that voice. Goddammit, don't tell me I got outta my bed for a skunk named Lobo McRae?'

Lobo swore softly as he stood beside his horse, hands raised shoulder high. Three men came out of the bunkhouse, guns trained on the trio.

'Who you got with you, Lobo? Nate says there's a woman.'

'And I'd appreciate it if you didn't label *me* a skunk, Bryce,' Beth called.

There was a general silence, enough for them to hear Bryce McCall's sharp intake of breath.

'Now what in the *hell* could bring you here in the middle of the night, Mrs Landis? No! Leave it till you come inside an' surprise me some more.' The shotgun barrel moved and Gunn paused as he dismounted. He lifted his hands warily.

'I'm the one'll surprise you, McCall. You don't know me – yet.'

'No-o-o. But let's change that. Come on in, all of you.

I'm almighty curious.' He raised his voice slightly. 'You boys stay out here with the hosses. *Anyone* comes outta the house an' it ain't me – shoot 'em down!'

As the trio stepped cautiously up on to the dark porch Bryce McCall moved back from the door, shotgun butt braced against his hip, and said, 'Welcome to Half-Moon, folks – and that's as friendly as I get till you do some talkin'.'

Bryce McCall looked a very tough customer. Rugged, work-worn, clothes a mite ragged or roughly patched, suggested there were no women on Half-Moon.

He had a stern face and his eyes were unwavering as he looked at the trio of unexpected visitors. He scratched his unshaven jowls and sat down in a hardback chair, lifting it dexterously on to the rear legs, using his own leg muscles as springs to rock slightly back and forth.

Two of his ranch hands stood by the door; tough cattlemen, holding guns down at their sides, but shoulders tensed, ready to use their weapons on the word from their boss.

McCall sniffed and the bristly hairs showing at his flaring nostrils twitched. He flicked a gnarled finger at Beth, who had removed her slicker now, then at Lobo.

'You I know – and you.' The somewhat chilling gaze settled on Gunn. 'You, I dunno, but if you're who I think you are I don't want to know you.' His gaze returned to Beth.

'He's Zack Gunn. As far as Murray and his men are concerned he's a long-lost brother of mine.'

McCall's eyes didn't waver from Gunn's deadpan face. 'You been doin'a mite of fibbin', girl?'

'Just – temporizing. You see, I called him Zack but he has lost his memory.' McCall snorted here, shaking his head slowly. 'It's true. He got mixed up with Creedy and Devlin. Charges were trumped up and—'

'I heard talk.' McCall's voice cut off her explanation. 'I don't want him here on Half-Moon. You neither, come to that. Nor you, Lobob. I still think you runnin'-ironed them three cows of mine last season.'

Lobo stared right back, saying nothing.

'I think you might want me, if not the others, Bryce,' Beth said. She walked over to a cluttered table with a propped-up leg that obviously served as McCall's desk. 'I want to write something.'

'There's pen and paper there somewhere.' McCall took out a battered cheroot from his ragged shirt pocket and fired up as the girl rummaged, found what she wanted sat down and began to write quickly. He frowned as he blew a long stream of smoke. 'What the hell you writin'?'

She signed for him to be patient, finished, and waved the paper for a moment to dry the ink a little. Then she handed it to him.

'I'll sign that here and now, under certain conditions.'

McCall's heavy lips moved as he read the words, then his head snapped up. He blinked with obvious surprise. 'You. . . . What the hell's behind this?' He tapped the paper hard. '*You* givin' me permission to drive my herds across your land to them canyons beyond? Now . . . wait up: what "conditions"?'

Beth, her face showing a little strain, nodded to the paper. 'I'll sign that if you agree to hide Zack.'

The rancher's jaw dropped. 'What. . . ?'

'Beth!' Gunn said sharply. 'I don't want you committing yourself to something like this.'

Without looking at him she waved his protest aside. 'What d'you say, Bryce? You want the deal or not?'

'Big question!'

'Takes but a small answer: yes or no.'

'I go along with Gunn, Beth,' Lobo spoke up suddenly. 'You give McCall right of way and he'll take it all the time.'

'I can put a time limit on it.'

'For once I agree with Lobo here,' McCall said, obviously seeing he had an advantage.

'Why would you want it all the time?' Beth asked. 'You claim it's better feed and water in those canyons and that you can fatten your herds by market time a lot faster if I allow you to use the graze. That's what I had in mind when I decided to offer you the deal.'

McCall's mouth twitched and Gunn knew it was his attempt at a smile – something the man rarely did, he figured. 'Sure, and that's right. But long as we're hoss-tradin'. . . .'

Before Beth could speak, Lobo said, 'He ain't so interested in packin' the meat on his cows – though that's a bonus – as he is in *hidin'* his herd.' They all looked at him puzzledly, except McCall, whose jaw jutted aggressively. 'Don't you get it? Reconstruction's just brought in a new cattle-head tax, double what it used to be. McCall's wantin' to hide out half his cows an' won't declare 'em

101

when the tax collector comes.'

McCall's eyes narrowed. 'You always did have the bad habit of pokin' your nose in where it don't belong, Lobo. You better watch out: it could get you killed.'

Lobo smiled crookedly, looking round at the others. 'Witnesses just heard you make that threat, McCall.'

'Threat? Hell, just offerin' you some advice.'

'Call it what you will,' Beth cut in sharply. 'Do you want me to sign that authority or not? I will – once I have your word you'll hide Zack and keep him safe until the hunt for him dies down.'

'Could be a long time,' mused the rancher, but he knew he had a good deal here. 'OK. You got my word.'

Beth was surprised when he offered one of his big, work-worn hands. Her own slim one seemed to be swallowed by it when they shook briefly. Then she signed the paper and McCall snatched it away quickly, grinning, showing a gap or two in his yellowed teeth. And she knew with a knotting of her stomach, that she had acted just a little too hastily. She should have pushed her own advantage while she had it. Now. . . .

'Beth, you shouldn't do this,' Gunn started to say. 'It's—'

'What I want,' she finished for him, smiling a trifle tightly. 'You took a big risk just to return Burton's jacket to me when you didn't even know me. You don't realize just how much that meant to me, Zack.'

Her voice trailed off and McCall cut in, folding the paper now and placing it in a worn leather wallet that he took from a hip pocket.

'No time for that soft soap. I got arrangements to

make, and I reckon a deal of tracks to cover. I don't want Murray or Killen followin' your trail in here. Come on, you. Gunn, eh? Well, I'm gonna be the one pullin' your trigger for quite a spell, mister. Best get used to takin' orders from me.'

Gunn merely returned the hard stare. The rancher gestured to his two men. 'See the girl and Lobo on their way while I figure out where to stash this ranny.'

'It had better be a good hiding-place, Bryce!'

McCall shrugged. 'I reckon I've got a few spots'll suit. But I'll do the choosin'.'

Beth frowned: she didn't care for his tone.

He was telling her he held the advantage now, and that Zack Gunn was the pawn in this deal, whatever she thought.

If he didn't get all that he wanted, McCall could threaten to bring in Murray and hand Gunn over to him. She was wide open to blackmail: should've made him give her a written guarantee that he wouldn't pull such a double-cross. Not that he would keep his word.

She had been aware of this while in the act of signing the paper, of course, but there hadn't seemed to be any choice at the time.

Now, Gunn didn't have any choice – about his life or where it was taking him.

Bitterly, she thought that he ought to be used to it by now. But he looked impassive: allowing himself to be manipulated simply because he had no past as a reference point, and little future that he could foresee.

Poor devil!

CHAPTER 11

HIDE AND SEEK

Bryce McCall sat down on a form by the table in the bunkhouse, scantily lit by two oil lamps. He tossed his cheroot pack across and Gunn took one. McCall let him light it from a vesta while he lit his own from the chimney of the nearer lamp.

'That gal – she can be a spitfire.'

Gunn said nothing, smoked slowly.

'She's been pushed around some, 'specially after Landis went missin'. He'd left her poorly provided for. Spent too much on land he couldn't afford. Like them canyons. Everyone expected her to sell and quit the county.'

'You most of all.'

McCall blew smoke, his face impassive. 'You got a lotta luck, her takin' a shine to you this way. She wouldn't stick her neck out for anyone else I know.' His face tightened. 'OK. Deal is for me to hide you. So, you help the boys

104

take my herd into them canyons and earn your keep.'

'OK by me, but I don't recollect if I even know how to work cows.'

McCall stared a long time, then smiled crookedly. 'Still pushin' that "lost your memory" deal, huh?'

'Look, McCall, quit the hasslin'. I've – lost – my – memory. That's it.'

The rancher pursed his lips. 'Mebbe. But you'll be all right workin' cattle.' He took a long drag on his cheroot, blew out smoke slowly before adding, 'You managed OK on your own spread near Socorro, before the war.'

Gunn froze, petrifying all movement, staring; smoke trickled from his nostrils. He swallowed, the sound clearly audible above the snores and coughs of the Half-Moon cowboys sleeping at the far end of the bunkhouse.

He made as if to stand, then dropped back on to the form. His voice was hoarse when he asked: 'You . . . know me?'

McCall blew more cheroot smoke. 'We've met.'

Gunn's hands bunched into fists on the table as he leaned across. 'Then tell me who the hell I am.'

'Why don't you leave it at Zack Gunn? Just ride clear of New Mexico and you'll be OK.'

Gunn frowned. 'Wh – what the hell did I do there?'

'Killed a sheriff: no damn loss, mind. Lousy lawman. Corrupt. Had a lot of enemies. Come to think of it, some of them'd likely hide you out for doin' what they were scared to do.'

Gunn cleared his throat. 'Tell me.'

'We'll call you "Laredo". You always claimed to come from there, and that's the monicker everyone knew you by. You joined the army; I was filling in as enlistment clerk. I seen your papers. Said your father was some kinda Limey from a place with a weird name, like a soup or somethin'. Yeah, that's it: Ar-broth, near enough. He had an accent you could cut with a knife. Most folk had trouble understandin' him. Likely some rubbed off on you and killed much of your Southern accent.'

'It's *Arbroath*, a town in Scotland, not England. Fishing place, up north, near Aberdeen.'

Gunn jumped as McCall waved his words away and the cheroot burned down to his fingers. He stabbed it out in the coffee-can lid, which was already overflowing with the crew's butts.

'How the hell did I know that!' he whispered shakily.

'Ain't important. Anyway, he and your mother were both dead when you signed up – died in a house fire. Nothin' suspicious.'

Gunn merely stared, waiting, hands still fisted up.

'You and the lawman were courtin' the same gal, Kitty Lee. Sheriff figured to frame you for rustlin', get under your neck that way. Tried to convince the gal but she stuck with you. He went crazy, beat her up, raped her. . . .'

'And. . . ?' Gunn's voice was barely audible.

McCall shrugged. 'You called him out in Socorro. Shot him to pieces, little at a time, made him crawl the whole length of Main Street to her grave with five of your bullets in him. He was dyin' anyway, but you put your last shot into him and rode out.'

Gunn's breath hissed through pinched nostrils; there was not a movement from him except the rise and fall of his chest. 'The gal? I – I don't recollect her. . . .'

'She was a looker.' That was all the rancher said but it was enough. Gunn's teeth made a grinding sound.

'War had started by then. You joined up. No problems, long as a man could walk upright and was strong enough to carry a musket, he was accepted.'

'How did you and me meet?'

'Like I said, I was temporary enlistment clerk.'

'How'd you know all this about the sheriff and so on?'

'You wasn't what they call a teetotaller in them days and we shared a coupla wingdings; did a few patrols together, too. Both good shots, used us as sharpshooters to knock down Yankee officers in the field.' McCall stubbed out his cheroot butt. 'We weren't exactly pards, but we had a coupla heart-to-hearts; you know a lot about me, too.'

'Not now I don't.'

'Might come back.' He shrugged again. 'But one time we were trapped in a dead-end canyon and figured we were all through – only a few bullets between us, Yankees crawlin' all over the countryside, and we'd picked off a whole bunch of their officers. So they rushed us. Left me for dead. Later I found out they took you – bein' a sergeant – to some prison camp the Yankees always say never existed. Lots of stories about torture of Reb officers.'

'Sierra Five!'

'See? Your memory's comin' back.'

Gunn shook his head. 'No. That's as far back as I go, just before the end of the war. I came to with Murray mistakin' me for Captain Landis, and then they blew a

107

mountain down on the camp. Must've thought I was dead, too. I'd hit my head somewhere, on a rock, I guess. Maybe that was when I lost my memory. Still dunno my real name.'

McCall frowned, poked at the overflowing coffee-tin lid, spilling cigarette butts on the tabletop. 'We all called you Laredo at that time, like I said.'

Gunn bared his teeth. 'Dammit, someone must've used my real name. Officers – other soldiers. Hell, you must've known it, bein' the recruitin' officer.'

'Uh-huh.' The rancher stared, body rigid now. 'But generally, you was just called "Sarge" or "Laredo".'

Gunn's frown deepened. 'Why the hell you makin' such a song and dance about this? If you know my name, for Chris'sake tell me!'

The rancher remained silent, tightlipped.

'Goddammit, McCall! What's the big mystery!'

Gunn was becoming more and more agitated. Then the rancher said quietly,

'Well, your name was – still is, I guess. . . .' He paused until he saw the dangerous look in Gunn's eyes, and said with a rush: 'Bryce McCall!'

A silence that seemed to make Gunn's ears feel as if they were being blown out from inside his head settled on the bunkhouse. Even the snoring cowpokes fell silent – for a little time, it seemed.

The man at present known as Zack Gunn started to rise out of his seat, his right hand moved across his body to the forward-facing butt of the Remington sidearm.

He froze, body raised only a few inches from the hard

108

form. The muzzle of the rancher's six-gun was visible above the edge of the scarred table and his eyes were narrowed. 'Just take it easy!'

Gunn slowly sat down, placing his hands on the edge of the table in full view. 'You making some kinda joke?'

The rancher shook his head. 'No. I thought you were dead. You see, I got clear of that canyon, by playin' dead, and decided I'd had a bellyful of the Army.'

'In other words, you deserted.' There was no disapproval or otherwise in Gunn's low voice.

'That's what I done, but a man my age and size at that time should've been wearin' some kinda uniform and I got pulled up by one of our own patrols, askin' why not? Had to give a name quick, and I used yours. Told them Chet Rowan – which was me – had been killed in that canyon. No one bothered to check, I guess. Damn war was finished a few weeks later anyway, and I had a perfectly good background by callin' myself Bryce McCall.'

'Who, I figure, was still wanted for killin' that Socorro sheriff?'

The rancher smiled crookedly. 'Man, the war was over! After six years of blood and fightin' no one cared about some jealous, crooked lawman who got what he deserved. Anyway, you gotta remember who won the war.'

Gunn nodded slowly. Sure. The Yankees wouldn't bother themselves with such things when they had Reconstruction to enforce.

'I don't recollect any of this. Like I said, my memory don't go back any further than when Murray found me in a ditch outside Sierra Five. But you've stole what's left

109

of my life, you son of a bitch!'

The six-gun barrel rapped the table edge sharply, getting Gunn's attention. 'I'm usin' your name, that's all, and I'm protectin' your hide from the Yankees. Don't forget that. You oughta be a mite more grateful.'

Gunn stared hard at him for a long minute. He saw it was starting to get to the rancher: beads of sweat were on the man's forehead. He licked his lips several times. His gunhand must have been sweating, too, for he worked the fingers around the six-gun butt almost constantly.

'All I gotta do is pull this trigger.'

'Mebbe you'd be doin' me a favour,' replied Gunn.

'Eyewash! You don't mean that. You've had some tough scrapes, sure, but no worse'n a lotta others. You can't tell me you ain't glad to be alive.'

Gunn remained silent, thinking about that.

'You call this livin'?' he asked at last.

It was only about six miles to the canyon country. Mostly the drive was across Beth's land which, to Gunn's mind, looked entirely separate from the farmland. To him it seemed like typical cattle country: hard, dusty, dotted with sotol and chaparral, sun-blasted rocks jutting here and there; more like New Mexico than Colorado.

He stopped his mount so suddenly that one of McCall's – *Rowan*'s – men almost collided with him. The cowpoke cussed him loudly and vehemently, like a Waco muleskinner with a burr under him. Gunn refused to think of the rancher as McCall. Hell, he had to hang on to something that was a real part of him, didn't he? Even if he was guessing which was which?

He started to ride again, then slowed; he felt his heart hammering. A 'Waco muleskinner'? Where did that come from?

He felt a slight shudder pass through his whip-lean body. Was his memory starting to return?

For the remainder of the drive he worked the cattle without conscious thought. Often he was the first to spot trouble brewing among the jostling steers, about 150 in all, and he rode in several times to nip things in the bud before they got out of hand.

If there was a breakaway he was on it in seconds, thundering up alongside with coiled rope swinging across the snorting nostrils as horns tried to rake him forcing the steer around towards the main herd. Another became bogged in a stream when the bank crumbled; it sank belly-deep into the ooze, bawling its head off in panic.

While cursing cowhands unshipped their lariats and began shaking out loops, Gunn leapt from his dun, ran to the bank, grabbed the steer's flailing tail and yanked it up straight, lifting to his toes, reaching as high as he could. The tail hardened like an iron rod, clear down to the butt. Straining, Gunn kicked the cow with his boot toe, just under the tail root. There was a sudden wild flurry, with mud flying, and the rear end of the steer burst clear. Experienced cowhands dropped their loops over the horns or a rear leg, uttering some of the most imaginative swearing Gunn had ever heard. The animal fell on its side and was dragged out. Gunn sourly wiped mud from his face and clothes as the others grinned.

'Looks jus' like the nigra boy we had workin' in our kitchen before the war,' commented a rawboned ranny

111

in a broad South Carolina accent.

While the other hands within hearing guffawed, the ramrod, Sandy Kern, rode up, nodding. 'Good work. Laredo. Is that what the boss called you?'

'Near enough. Or you can call me Gunn.'

'Sounds downright intimidatin'. You're a good hand, whatever name you go by. Why don't you get yourself a notebook an' write all them names down so you don't get mixed up?'

'Reckon I might at that.'

Gunn was pleased: it had been a long time since he had experienced the rough camaraderie of a trail drive – *a long time.* But the ghost of such a memory was stirring.

By the time they reached the labyrinth of canyons he realized he hadn't felt so relaxed in months. This was work he knew, something that came naturally to him.

It was a good feeling.

It was the kind of life he felt he was really suited to, where he 'belonged' might be a better way of putting it.

Well, he had a chance to try it now – provided Rowan kept his word.

CHAPTER 12

WOLF'S HOWL

'You shouldn't've gotten yourself into a spot like this, Beth – Not for someone like Gunn.'

Beth jumped: it was early morning and she was emptying the dishwater from washing up the breakfast things when Lobo appeared around the corner of the cabin. She held the dripping metal bowl and, heart hammering, snapped,

'What're you doing, sneaking around here! Good Lord! Have you been out here all night?'

'Just keepin' my word to the cap'n.'

'I've told you before, there's no need for you to do this, Lobo. You've got your own place to look after, I can manage.'

Lobo lit one of his cheroots and shook his head as he waved out the match flame. 'Not now you got Half-Moon crossin' your land, with your blessin'. You've give McCall freedom to come'n' go as he pleases.'

'He only has right of way to the canyons. For a limited time.'

Lobo smiled crookedly as he detected the uncertainty in her voice. 'You know damn well he won't stick to it. Hell, give him an inch, he'll take a mile – and a half!'

'Just leave me alone, Lobo. I have enough worries without you elaborating on them.'

'Beth, look. McCall can twist that permission to cross your land any way he wants. It was a stupid move.'

Her teeth tugged briefly at her full bottom lip. 'I – I just didn't see any other way to give Zack some protection. If Murray's men find him they'll. . . .'

She stopped, not knowing exactly what they would do. But from past performances, when a Reconstruction posse hunted someone who had broken their laws, well, not many came back alive. And there was a noose already hanging over Gunn's head.

'You know what'll happen. Not that it'll bother me any.'

'What else could I do?' she asked, a slight tremor of desperation in her voice now. 'I felt I owed him something for coming all this way with Burton's jacket, and with no memory of who he is.'

'Aah, if he's really lost his memory, he likely came hopin' you'd take pity on him, and you fell for it.'

She gripped the bowl hard by its rim. 'Lobo, it's no business of yours. No matter what you think you're doing. Anyway, it's done now and – and I just hope Zack will be able to get clean away when the manhunt dies down.'

'Reconstruction never gives up where Johnny Rebs're

concerned. You oughta know that.'

'Well, they have to find him first. I – I believe Bryce McCall will stick to his word. He badly wants to hide at least half of his herds before the new head tax is enforced. Everyone knows he's hurting for money.'

Lobo's rugged face was set in hard lines. 'You shoulda just handed Gunn over an' you'd have no worries.'

She frowned. 'Why do you dislike him so much?'

Lobo shrugged easily. 'He's still just a Reb to me. An' I don't want him pokin' his nose into my business.'

'*Your* business?'

'Told you, the cap'n saved my neck an' I give him my word to watch out for you – an' that's what I'm gonna do, Beth.' He touched a finger to his hatbrim, started to turn away to where he had left his mount with trailing reins on the other side of the well. Then swung back. 'Whether you like it or not.'

She started to retort but decided against it. Squinting a little as the sun's light strengthened, she watched him mount his big black and ride off, flicking his half-smoked cheroot into the well as he did so.

The horse moved steadily across the yard and her teeth once again tugged at her bottom lip.

She had never really felt at ease with Lobo, but, somehow, this latest confrontation had shaken her worse than usual.

If she had felt uneasy dealing with Lobo, her next visitors made her feel positively ill.

They came in a ragged column: the size of the dust cloud immediately set her heart pounding and stomach churning. There must be at least twenty riders! All armed.

Major Murray himself led the search party, which was only one of several that she knew about. He was barely courteous, sitting his dusty mount in the shade of the cabin, nodding curtly. 'We're looking for Zachariah Gunn, or whatever he calls himself. But I believe you're aware of that already.'

She had been baking to keep herself busy. Now she used a few taut seconds to get herself under control, wiping her floury hands carefully on a ragged-edged tea towel.

'Why would I think that? You have him locked up in your jail, don't you?'

Murray's face could have been chipped out of granite. 'Perhaps it's because I think you helped him escape.'

She gasped, reared back. '*Escape?* My God, I never heard of anyone escaping from that fortress you call a local jail!' She paused, trying to figure out just how Murray would expect her to react to such news. She allowed a crooked half-smile to touch her lips. 'But if Zack somehow pulled off that kind of – miracle – then I'm not sorry to hear it. As for me helping him, that's plain ridiculous.'

Murray's eyes narrowed. He nodded to Killen, who dismounted and gestured for four troopers to go search the barn. Killen smirked at Beth. 'Won't mind if we check your cabin, too, will you?'

He thrust by without waiting for an answer. One soldier followed him inside. Her eyes blazed as she looked back at Murray. 'You have no right to do this, Major!'

'I have every right as a deputy commissioner of the Reconstruction. Mrs Landis, one of the witnesses said he thought there was a woman involved in the jailbreak, wearing a long poncho as disguise.'

'I think we just found it, Major. Hangin' in full view.'

They turned as Killen held up the long slicker, which Beth had hung back on its usual wall peg after returning home last night. She hadn't noticed the smear of tar on one flap at the bottom and Killen gave her a smug, unsmiling look as he indicated it.

'Big barrel back of the jailhouse. Looks just like a rain-water butt. Might've been once, but now it's half-full of tar for waterproofing the shingles on the jailhouse roof. Tar oozed a little through the seams of the barrel staves, it bein' out in the sun and weather. A poncho flapping around someone's legs could easily pick up a smear like this one.'

Beth was silent briefly, then looked defiantly, first at Killen, then Murray. 'Yes, I know it can happen. Strangely enough, I have had the same thought about waterproof-ing my shingles before the rainy season begins.' She gestured to the split and misplaced ones above the doorway. 'If you care to look in my barn, you'll find I have a small half-keg of tar and it, too, has leaked through the staves. They have also opened slightly because of the long dry spell we're having. Go ahead. Take a look. I wore my slicker so I wouldn't get any tar on my clothes while I painted the shingles.'

They soon satisfied themselves she was telling the truth – at least about the leaky half-keg – and some shin-gles had been daubed with tar. Murray's face flushed and it was obvious that Killen was swearing bitterly to himself. Tar was tar – they couldn't prove exactly where it came from.

'I'm wondering why you came here, Major. Did you by any chance find some tracks that could've been made by Zack Gunn leading to my door? You must've had a very *good* reason, surely. You wouldn't just come here to harass me, would you?'

Murray looked like he wanted to hit her; he lifted his reins as he signed to Killen to call back the barn searchers.

'I know you helped Gunn get out of that jail. Being a hero's widow won't save you when I can prove it.'

'And when d'you think that'll be, Major?' Beth almost flutttered her eye lashes at him, but pulled up short: she had made him angry enough.

'As soon as the word spreads that there is now an authorized bounty of three thousand dollars on Gunn's head.' He smiled slightly as he saw her face turn white. 'You know, Mrs Landis, folk around here are mostly poor. Not many – if *any* – would pass up the chance to claim that much money.' He started to rein around, but paused long enough to add, 'That's dead or alive, by the way.' He touched his hand to his hatbrim once more. 'Good day to you, ma'am.'

She somehow stood there, hands knotted behind her back, and looked as implacable as she could while the column rode carelessly through her vegetable and flower gardens, knocked over one set of posts supporting the clothes' line and generally made one hell of a din as they left the yard.

Her weak legs carried her back into the cabin. She collapsed on to the nearest chair, leaned her elbows on the table's edge and allowed a shudder of fear to pass through her body.

Something warm splashed on to the back of one hand. When she looked down she saw it was made by a falling tear. Three thousand dollars' bounty! Gunn wouldn't stand a chance once the word got out.

It was near sundown when a rider came into the canyon camp from Half-Moon headquarters, bringing grub supplies on a packhorse,

It was obvious to Gunn that Chet Rowan figured to keep his herds in these canyons for as long as possible, so he intended to get his men settled in.

As far as the rancher was concerned Gunn didn't fit into his plans anywhere at this stage, so for the present he would leave him here with the cowhands who were already settling down the herd for the night behind a hastily thrown-up brush fence.

'Boss said to tell you Monte'll be along with the wagon tomorrow,' the new arrival told Kern, helping himself to some stew they had brought from the ranch and reheated.

Kern nodded. Gunn paused with a dripping spoon halfway to his mouth. 'A wagon – of what?' he asked.

Kern looked at him sharply. 'Aw – supplies to see us through.'

'How long do you figure to be here?'

'Long as the boss says. Now, don't worry about it, Laredo. You'll be safe enough here.'

119

'It was meant to be for just a few days, or a week. This sounds like McCall's plannin' on movin' in permanent.'

Kern chewed more meat from the stew before answering. 'Well, I guess that's up to the boss. We just do what we're told.' The ramrod gave Gunn a steady look. 'You should, too. Be a lot easier in the long run.'

Gunn turned quickly to the man who had brought the extra food supplies. 'What's that wagon bringin'?'

The man shrugged his burly shoulders. He had been called 'Curly' by Kern and the others but with his hat pushed back from his face, Gunn could see he was bald.

'Guess you'll just have to wait an' see.'

'No, I'm askin' you now.' Gunn looked around at the others, settled his gaze on the ramrod. 'I wondered why he sent you. You're gonna supervise somethin', ain't you? Maybe like throwing up a line camp? Squatting on Beth's land.'

Kern shrugged, but his eyes were wary. 'Boss's had his eye on this place for a long time. It's kinda sneaky, I guess, but hell – that widder-woman don't use this land.'

'Mebbe she has future plans.'

Kern smiled crookedly, spread his arms. 'Like I said, kinda tough on her, but you gotta grab with both hands when you see somethin' you want these days.'

'You're not making me part of this.'

There was a general tensing among the men round the campfire and Kern shrugged again.

'Oughta be grateful you got some place to hole up.'

'I am. Grateful to Beth Landis.'

Kern wiped his mouth with the back of his hand, eyes steady on Gunn. 'Mister whoever-you-are, things are all arranged. You accept 'em or not, makes no difference to me. But you stay put till you're told different'

Gunn's hard expression didn't change, but he thought: and let Half-Moon steal these canyons right out from under Beth. That sure didn't set right.

There were four of them, counting Curly, Gunn had all six chambers of the Remington loaded, with a spare cylinder in the belt pouch, which he'd also taken the trouble to load. Reliable self-contained cartridges for pistols were rare at that time, most were rimfire. Some Colts were already using them, but most of the war weapons were still percussion types. Gunn's Remington, the 1858 model, was one of them, firing either a combustible, self-consuming paper cartridge or one loaded directly into each chamber with loose powder and ball.

It was a laborious job, measuring the right charge of powder into each chamber, tamping a wad, ramming in the .44-calibre lead ball on top, then thumbing a percussion cap on to each of the six nipples on the cylinder base. Anyone with any sense carried a spare, fully loaded cylinder; when the gun emptied it was a simple matter to pull the release pin, dropping the empty cylinder, then swiftly replace it with the ready one.

Such attention to detail had saved many a life in a heated gunbattle. Following this method meant that he had twelve shots to take care of four men. Pretty good odds.

Reaching for the ladle in the bubbling stew, he suddenly kicked the iron pot in the direction of the others; three sat close together, Curly sat on a log, slightly separate. Men howled as the hot gravy and meat hit them.

Gunn reared to his feet, revolver in hand.

Curly somersaulted backward, his own six-gun in his hand, blazing. He was fanning the hammer spur, got off two fast shots but the third was a misfire – common with percussion pistols of that era. Muzzle loaders did not take kindly to fanning: either the crude mechamism simply couldn't match the speed, or the jolting loosened the percussion caps and caused misfires.

Gunn dived to one side. He snapped a shot at Curly, saw the man's right arm jerk violently and the gun go flying as Curly grabbed at his bloody wound. By then Kern and the others had their guns blazing.

Gunn rolled on to his belly, put two fast shots into the fire. Flaming debris erupted. Kern and his pards threw their arms across their faces and Gunn ran for the mounts. He vaulted into the saddle of the dun: earlier, he had drawn the short straw for first nighthawk duty and had saddled up, ready to ride down to the herd after supper.

Kern was yelling. Curly screamed something: he was on his knees, blood dripping from his wound. One of the others, Taggart, jumped up, running forward, pistol thrust out in front. His shots were wild. Gunn wheeled the dun and as the horse flashed past Gunn kicked Taggart in the chest. Taggart rolled into Kern and they fell in a cursing tangle. Gunn raced his mount into the shadows of the wall, hipped awkwardly and triggered. The hammer fell on an empty chamber. He rammed the gun back into leather and concentrated on getting clear of the canyon.

This was all strange country to him, but as long as he

was away from here it wouldn't really matter.

Kern and the others didn't know this country much better than he did. They knew this canyon, which McCall had wanted to use for a long time, well enough, but the twisted, rugged terrain beyond was just as strange to them as it was to Gunn.

With darkness fast closing down, he had some kind of a chance of getting away. But to where?

CHAPTER 13

BOUNTY HUNTERS

The shadows were thickening and Gunn was riding so fast that he almost skidded into a rock wall on a particularly sharp bend.

It scared the horse, which balked and snorted, whinnying as it stomped and fought the bit. In the confined space the sounds were amplified; he even heard them echoing from some doglegged arroyo close by.

If Kern and the others didn't hear this racket they would have to be deaf.

But instead of continuing to fight the dun he suddenly eased up on the reins and threw his weight to the right, so that the horse was guided towards the bend of the dogleg. The dun seemed happy enough to accept this and with a snort and a leap that rocked Gunn in the saddle, it ran for the bend. He let it have its head, knowing the horse would take the dogleg at a safe speed.

It did. He found himself in a deep gash through the

rocks. Glancing up he saw a few pinpoints of light that would soon be bright, twinkling stars.

Behind, he heard the thunder of hoofs and a couple of unintelligible yells as his pursuers searched for which way he had gone. Dust hanging in the air told them more than finding skid marks or hoofprints in this light.

They spurred forward, grim-faced, just three of them now: Curly had stayed behind to doctor his shattered arm.

Taggart thought he spotted Gunn. He reined up, lifted his carbine and loosed off two shots that thundered and slapped through the rock-walled cutting.

'Judas priest!' roared Kern, rubbing his ear on the left side, which had been closer to Taggart. 'You damn near deafened me.'

Taggart didn't answer; he jacked another shell into the Spencer's breech and urged his mount on ahead. Kern set his own mount going; the third man, Case, wheeled around him. All three turned into the dogleg bend and suddenly it was full of flying bullets, a couple striking sparks from the granite walls. Their mounts reared and swung against each other in the tight space. Case toppled from the saddle and Kern just managed to grab his saddle horn and keep from falling. Taggart's shoulder struck a jutting rock and he dropped his carbine, moaning as he grabbed the injured arm.

'Hell with this,' growled Kern. 'We'll wait till daylight. I go no notion to ride into a headshot.'

Case, breathless from his fall, limping, nodded agreement. Taggart was doubtful and said, 'I think I might've winged him.'

'You got owl eyes?' snapped the ramrod. 'You couldn't see well enough in this light to be sure.'

'I – I still think I hit him. Or his hoss. I'm gonna take a look.'

'Stubborn damn fool,' Kern muttered as Taggart rode slowly round the bend.

He and Case were smoking behind some rocks when the man came back. 'I was right! There's blood on some rocks. Good-sized splash, too. We might be able to track him a little longer.'

'No!' Kern growled. 'If he's hit bad, he won't make it very far. If it's his hoss you got, same thing: We wait till daylight.'

It was the dun that had been hit by Taggart's ricocheting bullet.

The lead had caromed off a part of the rock wall that slanted outwards, the angle driving it down as Gunn rammed his heels home and got the horse moving. If it had been stationary the bullet probably would have shattered its hip. As it was, responding to the rider's urging, the dun's rear end had swerved violently, the bullet searing diagonally down on the left hip. Blood sprayed on to the rocks and Gunn was almost thrown from the saddle as the horse swerved and twisted briefly before lunging awkwardly to one side.

Gunn expected more shots but they didn't come. He heard Kern's voice yelling that they would wait until daylight.

Which suited him. He would have time to dismount, examine the dun's wound and wash it, even rest up some. But he would have to get it moving before the hip stiffened too much.

Kern and the others made a cold camp amongst some boulders, sheltered by a rock jutting from one of the walls. Neither Case nor Taggart were happy about standing guard, but Kern was fair enough and took first duty.

There was nothing to alarm him and he slept most of his shift. Taggart found him dozing and made a promise to himself that he, too, would sleep his guard time away.

When Taggart's snoring woke Case and he couldn't get back to sleep he was angry enough to get up and wake Taggart roughly, then take over.

All three men were sleeping peacefully when Monte Chiles found them just after sunup.

'Wake up, you damn fools!' he bellowed, his voice echoing and booming around the walls.

The three men started up, fumbling for their guns, hearts hammering. Monte Chiles was a small man with a big voice and he grinned crookedly at their woozy antics as they cussed him out good.

'The boss won't be happy I tell him I found you three asleep.'

'Then don't tell him,' growled Case thickly, spitting and wiping a wrist across his mouth.

But Kern frowned. 'Why? Any reason why we shouldn't sleep?'

'Guess not, seein' as you dunno yet.'

All three looked at him, puzzled. 'Know what?'

Monte looked around and lowered his voice. 'That Murray's put a bounty on Gunn's head.' He paused for effect, having got their full attention now. 'Three thousand bucks!'

There was a stunned silence, then Taggart hissed, 'You're joshin'!'

Monte Chiles shook his head emphatically. 'Nah, nah. This is gospel. Murray's got a posse out, spreadin' the word. I was s'posed to leave at daylight with that wagonload of lumber for the line shack but I snuck out early.' He looked at them one at a time. 'I figured three thousand divided by four is still pretty good *dinero*. The boss never told Murray where Gunn was, so I figured we could get in first an'—'

'There's Curly,' Kern said quietly. 'That makes five.'

Monte winked. 'Sent him back to get his arm fixed.'

It took no time at all for them to make their deal. But they had to hurry and nail Gunn before McCall came looking himself.

Gunn hadn't moved far during the night.

The dun's hip wound was deeper than he'd thought and it stiffened sooner than expected. He had made a small fire, heated most of his canteen water, then soaked a spare shirt, holding it in place with the animal kicking and jerking until the heat started to give relief. Then the dun was more tractable.

Leading the limping horse across a slope, using the sparse brush for cover, Gunn was startled to find he had four men hunting him now. He stopped behind a good-sized bush, watching.

Taggart was down on one knee, holding his mount's reins as he studied the ground. Gunn hadn't taken a lot of time to cover his tracks because the dun was moving so slowly. They would pick up his trail soon enough.

He checked his ammunition, fully loaded the used cylinder but didn't thumb the percussion caps on to the nipples. They had a habit of falling off as the cylinder was fixed into the gun frame and it was safer to place them in position after the cylinder was locked in.

Even with the sun shining he couldn't be sure of the country he was traversing. He thought he had the direction right, but even though Beth had shown him the area on a map, he wasn't certain sure. It had looked like it would be easy to get lost, and now he hoped he wasn't.

He would just have to be content with staying ahead of the hunters, if he could. At the same time he had to consider the horse: being caught on foot in this tangle of rocks and crumbling walls was nothing to look forward to.

'There's the sonuver!'

It was Monte Chiles who spotted Gunn as he led the limping dun as fast as was safe across an opening between two high needle rocks, which were briefly though clearly silhouetted against a blue sky.

Taggart and Case both brought up their rifles and the booming thunder of the shots reverberated around the walls. Kern saw rock chips spurt high above Gunn's head. The man turned, grabbed the reins in both hands and it looked like he actually pulled the ailing mount the rest of the way across, into shelter behind the tallest of the needle rocks.

'Dammittohell!' spat Case.

'You'd've done better to hold your fire,' Kern snapped. 'We could've gotten ahead and above him if you hadn't been so damn trigger happy!'

'Well, standin' here cussin' us out won't get us no closer,' Taggart observed sourly. Kern bit back a retort but nodded curtly.

'Right. Get mounted and follow me. I know this section pretty good. We can corner him if he sticks to that trail. The way that dun looked, I don't reckon he'll risk takin' it down the slope.'

They were right: Gunn could see only one way down from this narrow ledge and he knew the dun would never make it. He would have to stick to this trail until it swung down naturally and hope it wasn't too steep for the horse.

That was supposing, of course, that McCall's men didn't pick him off first.

But he had cover now and he had to make full use of it. He wished he could mount and make more ground, but the dun wasn't up to anything like that: he was lucky the horse was behaving as well as it was. If the pain got too bad and it started fighting the reins on shaky rear legs they could both finish up at the bottom of the narrow canyon, just ugly red smears on the waiting rocks.

Five minutes later he knew they had him.

The ledge ended on a rough semicircle of rock, fairly flat but with a distinct lean one way, beyond which was a drop of twenty-some feet with no soft landing.

He pulled the panting horse in behind a low boulder, held the bridle short and tight, and tried to calm it down with soothing talk while his eyes roved the country below.

'Goddamn!'

Even as he said the word he saw them, on a wide ledge across a draw with plenty of shelter from rocks and a few bushes. He ducked instinctively as two guns fired and the horse stomped and whickered as rock chips showered over them both.

'No place to go, Gunn!' called Kern.'No need to get yourself shot up. Just come on down with your hands up. We'll even take care of the hoss.'

Gunn was silent for a spell and after Kern's second appeal – only slightly more blunt – he frowned. Then he raised his voice:

'Why you doin' this, Kern? It ain't just about me wanting to see Beth Landis gets a fair deal. There's somethin' else, ain't there?'

The silence from across the draw dragged on and he knew he was right: there was some other reason they were hounding him. Curly had deserved what had happened to him; the others had reacted more or less like he'd expect from saddle mates, but there was something different in Kern's voice now.

Then he knew.

Kern called, 'We can do it easy – or the other way. The bounty says "dead or alive".'

Bounty! Hell, Murray must've decided he could capture Gunn faster by putting up a reward – and it would work, too! Nothing like money in a cash-strapped county to bring out the man-hunters.

Reconstruction was meant to get the country back on its feet, but there was still too much hatred between

North and South for any good intentions to be accepted. The men who were charged with getting things into order often let their predjudices rule their judgement.

Sometimes they were desperate enough to put up a bounty so that they could have their way. A bounty that would tempt folk to even betray their own kin.

Without conscious thought he brought up the Spencer and got off three fast shots, seeing the men across the draw scatter in alarm, rock dust flying, one of the bushes shaking as lead clipped the branches.

'You want that bounty, you sons of bitches, you're gonna have to earn it:' he called.

CHAPTER 14

RESCUER

The bounty hunters sent back a volley that chewed rock out of the ledge. It was deadly enough to make the already injured horse whinny and rear up. Because of the hip wound, the leg on that side would not take its weight and the dun crashed into the crouching Gunn, sending him sprawling.

He lost his grip on the Spencer and it fell over the edge, skidding for a short distance before striking a rock and tumbling end over end out of sight.

'That workin' hard enough to suit you?' called Taggart, crowing like a rooster so as to rub it in.

But he ducked fast enough when Gunn's Remington tracked him and the slug tore the hat from his head.

'Judas! The sonuver's a damn good shot!' breathed Kern. 'Spread out. He's still stuck on that ledge and his ammo won't last.'

'Won't have to, he shoots any straighter,' Case growled.

'Well, he ain't shootin' at all now, so I reckon you're right about him gettin' low on ammo,' Taggart said, poking his finger through the bullet hole in his recovered hat. 'Hell, just a mite lower an' I wouldn't be needin' a hat – nor nothin' else!'

Monte had moved a couple of yards along now and squeezed himself into a space between two boulders. One was just chest high and he was able to settle his Henry repeater firmly against his shoulder while resting his elbows on the rock.

There was a slight movement of the brush up there and Monte fired instantly. The brush swayed violently and Case said, excited, jumping up from behind his own shelter:

'You got him! You nailed him, Monte—'

The Remington hammered and Case spun away, down on his knees, clutching his chest high up, his head hanging.

'Damn fool!' Kern muttered. 'You're the one got nailed. How bad?'

Case's head was swaying and he looked up, grey-faced, his spread hand just below his right shoulder, blood running between the fingers. 'Bad – enough.'

Taggart was at his side, hunkered down, nervously checking to make sure his head was below the rocks, prising the hand away. Blood spurted and he tore off his neckerchief, wadded it and jammed Case's hand on top of it.

'Hold it there. It's bad, but not too bad,' he told Kern.

134

'He won't die. Unless he bleeds to death.'

Kern's mouth was a tight slit now as he turned to look across to Gunn's ridge. 'All right. He's set the deal. We take the bastard in *dead*!'

They lifted their guns and fired a raking, crashing volley that slammed through the hills like the first rumble of a summer thunderstorm. The bullets made Gunn flatten himself against the rocks. He was surprised when the dun jumped over him and a line of low boulders he had thought marked the limit of this ledge. He heard it fall, but then it was snorting and whickering as it got to its feet over there and clattered awkwardly away to shelter he hadn't been aware of.

But when he tried to get over the line of boulders too, the hunters raked his shelter with another volley and he fell flat, as lead hammered and whined and rock chips stung him.

'We got no argment with the hoss, Laredo! But you stay put!'

Another burst of fire came hard on Kern's shouted words and Gunn knew he would be lucky to live through a third volley. Squinting through the lower part of the now shredded bush he saw they had moved a few feet higher, giving them a better view of his ledge.

One of the rifles down there – he thought it was the Henry by the sharp crack it made – sent a bullet so close that he felt the warmth of its air-whip an instant before the lead laid a silver-grey streak over the rock and kicked grit against his face. Instinctively he rolled away from it, rammed himself up against an unyielding rock. He was exposed now, through the bullet-blasted bush, and he threw himself desperately aside even as the guns below fired. Something jarred his upper body, flinging him into an awkward sprawl. His pistol skidded from his hand. 'Damn those undersized grips!' He scrabbled for the weapon, whipped his hand back as lead burned across the back of it, barely breaking the skin but making his fingers tingle.

He lay there then, most of his upper body exposed, and thought: *Well, this is it. You die without even knowing who the hell you really are.* He briefly wondered if it made any real difference, anyway. *No! Dead is dead.*

He was tensed, prepared to meet the shock of bullets – there were guns hammering in a vicious volley now – but no lead was clanging or whining off his shelter. *What the hell. . . ?*

He had a blurred image of his attackers across there on their ledge and he gaped as he saw Case spin violently and lurch forward, dropping over the ledge without a sound, his rifle and hat falling separately. Behind and a little above Case's falling body, Taggart sat down hard, knocked from his squatting position, bent to the left as he clamped a hand to his bleeding side.

Kern and Monte – although he didn't know the latter's name – pushed swiftly backward and dropped out of sight. Then a pair of hands reached up and grabbed Taggart's ankles, dragging him under cover.

'You want to live – mount up and ride *now!*' bawled a voice from higher up on the slope above the wounded men.

Gunn's ears were ringing with all the gunfire and he didn't recognize the voice, but who cared? Whoever it was had saved his neck – had even sounded like he was on his side!

He stayed put, breathing hard, waiting for his rescuer to make his move. While the man apparently watched to see if Kern and his men were leaving, Gunn released the empty cylinder from his pistol, fumbled out the fully loaded spare and managed to clip it into place before his rescuer stood up, holding a Henry repeater rifle, pointed in his direction. By feel, he pushed the percussion caps on to the cylinder's nipples, one by one.

'You can crawl out of your hidy-hole now. They gone. Hope you din' wet your pants!'

The man laughed harshly. Gunn holstered the Remington and stood slowly, hands raised as he stared at the tightly grinning Lobo McRae.

'You look kinda surprised,' Lobo chuckled, the rifle unwavering.

'Well, I never expected *you*'d save my life.'

'Aw, 't'weren't nothin'. See, I din't *exactly* save your life I aim to kill you anyway.'

Gunn frowned. 'I don't get it. You might as well have let Kern an his pards finish the job for you.'

'Aw, no! I want to do it myself. My birthday tomorrow, see, and you're my present to me.'

Gunn remained silent for a long minute. 'That's kinda – loco, ain't it?'

Lobo shrugged his big shoulders. 'Depends how you look at it. See, I'll tell Beth you was killed by Kern and his pards, that I was just too late to save your neck, but I'll claim the re-ward."

'So you heard about it, and come ahunting.'

137

'Hell, why not? I can use the money. Beth might even take more notice of me if I got cash to spend on her, help her get that lousy li'l farm into shape.' His voice took on a strange, plaintive edge. 'She'll see I ain't such a bad catch, an' when I convince her the cap'n ain't never comin' back – well, she's a real lady, you know. She'll do the right thing and show her appreciation by marryin' me.'

Gunn went very still. *The poor soppy sonuver!* was his first thought. 'Beth's a real lady, all right,' Gunn said slowly. 'But as long as there's a chance Landis will show up some day she won't marry anyone. She don't really believe he's dead.'

Lobo's face twisted in anger and he shouted: 'He is! There ain't no chance of him comin' back, I tell you.' Lobo was emphatic and Gunn could see his eyes were wide and wild. 'An' no chance you'll be around to take her from me, neither.'

'Hey, whoa! I'm not making any kind of a play for Beth. I was just hoping she might be able to help me find out who I really am.'

Lobo laughed briefly. 'Hell, *I* know who you are!'

Gunn stiffened. 'What're you saying?'

'Huh! I know you're some smart-talkin' Johnny Reb who's tryin' to get on Beth's good side. That woman, that *lady*, she's like a – an angel! So wonderful. Landis never deserved her. He had big notions, spent what little money he had buyin' this useless canyon country. Figured he could divert the river and make it all lush for his herds, while Beth handled the farmin' side.' He shook his head, spat. 'I was only his sergeant but I tried to tell him he was makin' a mistake: his plan was far too expensive. Wouldn't listen. Then we got caught in that Hellfire Bend thing, and he got hit. Took a bad one in the chest, just the two of us, Rebs comin' after us, and we was almost outta ammo – but so was the Rebs. I went down when it was dark and I got all three with my knife. When I got back the cap'n was real bad. I sat with him till daylight. He was goin', I could see that. Might've got him to our lines in time, but I was plumb tuckered, fell asleep. When I woke up he was dead.'

'Why did you say he was "missing" then?' Gunn was careful to keep his voice at a natural, enquiring level.

Lobo frowned, looked at Gunn as if he was only now aware of his presence. Then he raised the rifle to his shoulder. 'I figured Beth' d go into mournin' for Landis. No tellin' for how long. But if she thought he might turn up and I told her the cap'n got me to swear to watch out for her – well, she'd get used to me bein' around, and. . . .' He stopped and grinned. 'Well, the bounty on your head'll get me her for my wife.'

Gunn instinctively started to move his hand towards the Remington but stopped when Lobo suddenly laughed.

'Who you tryin' to bluff!' He shook his head disdainfully. 'You damn Rebs! Think all us Yankees are dumb. I watched you shoot it out with Kern's bunch. You got nothin' but an empty gun there. Counted your shots, see? Take you till next Tuesday week to reload that cylinder.' His voice hardened. 'Anyways, I never did like you.'

Gunn threw himself sideways, right hand drawing the

Remington smoothly from the holster even as Lobo fired the Henry rifle. The bullet snored close by the fast-moving Gunn's ear as he landed on his left shoulder and triggered, hoping none of the percussion caps had jarred loose.

Lobo jerked and took a wavering step backwards as the bullets slammed into him. His face was slack with surprise as he dropped to his knees, still clutching the smoking rifle. It jumped from his slackening grip as he fired it, and fell to the ground as he spread out face diwn. Blood ran from a corner of his mouth. He raised his head by some supreme effort and a hand reached out as if to touch Gunn way across the draw.

'T-tell Beth – I – done my best – to – look out – for her. Please! Wan' her – to think – well of me. . . .'

Gunn felt a wave of pity wash over him. As Lobo's head slumped once more he said, loud enough for the man to hear – if he was still able to hear:

'I'll do that, Lobo.' He added to himself, 'You poor, besotted bastard. You never had a chance with her. You couldn't see it. But you saved my neck, so . . . *adios.*'

He touched two fingers to his hat in a brief, farewell salute.

The arm movement made him wince as the chest muscles involved twitched in sharp pain. He felt himself gingerly, afraid one of the bounty hunters' bullets might have torn him up. He breathed easy when he realized it was only a fragment of rock that had penetrated his shirt and lodged just beneath the skin. There was even hardly any blood.

So, he was still active, and now he could take his time,

reloading the Remington's cylinders.

Last man standing – again!

'Must mean somethin',' he murmured, hopefully.

CHAPTER 15

KILLER

He dragged the bodies under a rock ledge and covered them with brush.

Already there were frustrated buzzards wheeling in the sky. He began a search for the roan, ignoring several mounts that had belonged to the dead men. He felt a special rapport with that roan, it had stood by him and now it had a wound, though not too serious: he figured it was only right that he should stand by it.

He whistled shrilly and the horse trotted out from some rocks, limping slightly, head tossing. Grinning, he rubbed its ears and under the long jaw, being nudged pretty roughly, but affectionately, in return. Then, taking Lobo's Henry, he reloaded it from the dead man's spare ammunition, dropping some extra rim-fire cartridges into his pocket before mounting.

He hadn't gone far when a rifle whipcracked and a bullet buzzed past his head like a hornet. He lifted the reins and picked out a big boulder to use as cover. Then Chet Rowan called down.

'Just stay put! Judas, you are one dangerous son of a bitch, ain't you? I'm short three men thanks to you. See you're headed in the direction of my ranch. What business you figure you got there?'

'None, now you're here.'

There was a short silence. 'Sounds kinda ominous.'

'Needn't be. Just want you to tear up that right-of-way authority Beth gave you.'

'Hah! I been tryin' to get that for months.'

'You got it. Now it's run out. Take my word for it.'

Rowan chuckled. 'Sassy bastard.' He was standing in full view, confident, rifle held across his lower body, ready to shoot. 'What'm I gonna do with you?'

'Reckon your only interest in me is a dollar sign in front of a figure three, followed by three zeros. Close?'

'You always was a quick thinker, Laredo. But not quite quick enough this time.' Even as he spoke his rifle swung up.

Gunn's Henry lifted in a blur of speed. Three shots rolled out in one long roar, and rock dust spurted into Rowan's face even as he triggered . . . too late! He jerked hard, throwing his shot wild. Gunn's next bullet burned across the rancher's neck. He clapped his hands to the wound, stumbled, fell, and began to writhe when he hit the ground. Next thing he knew, Gunn was standing over him with the smoking rifle muzzle held two inches from his sweating face.

'We're goin' back to your place. Wanna argue?'

*

143

After leaving Half-Moon, Gunn kept to back trails, thoughtfully marked by Beth on the map she had drawn in case he needed to leave the general area in a hurry.

He saw some riders in the distance, blue Union jackets moving darkly across the landscape. Murray had his patrols out, still searching. Gunn changed direction constantly. Soon he was deep in country that hadn't been marked on the map. But this whole area would be crawling with hopeful bounty hunters. The only thing in his favour was that most of them would be amateurs. Still, a hungry man reaching for what he figured as easy money could be mighty dangerous.

Every time he saw a rider, or even a patch of swirling dust that might indicate a rider, he got under cover, waited a spell before riding along his original trail or dodging and zigzagging until he figured he had confused any pursuer. And himself, too, more than half the time.

But he always had an eye on the sun and took his direction from it. As he passed some cliffs he glimpsed a vertical stream of silver; he was sure it was the waterfall that had concealed his cave. He knew where he was now. He arrived within sight of Beth's place by early afternoon.

He found some trees to give him shelter and sat the saddle, badly wanting a smoke, but he refrained. He studied the farm, saw Beth watering her trampled flowers, throwing a pile of ruined ones away. At the vegetable patch she salvaged what she could, almost filling an old flour sack.

He was about to come out of cover and ride in when

there was a swirl of dust and a clatter as a buckboard bounced over the rise and rolled to a stop near the front door.

The driver was Haviland from the Climax store: no mistaking that ball-like figure with a hat stuck on top.

Gunn took one final, careful look around and, satisfied there was no one lurking about, heeled the roan forward and rode at a jogtrot towards Beth's cabin, the Henry rifle across his thighs.

He wasn't sure who showed the most surprise – or alarm – at his appearance, the storekeeper or the girl.

He answered their questions quickly and succinctly. Then he turned to the girl, took a folded kerchief from his shirt pocket and handed it to her. 'Present for you.'

Puzzled, Beth unfolded the cloth and looked up sharply as the breeze disturbed a small pile of half-compressed charred paper. The flakes began to blow away.

Gunn said. 'That's the right of way you wrote out for McCall – or Rowan, if you want his real name. It's expired.'

'My God! What did you do to him?'

'He's kinda indisposed, and likely a long way from here by now. But he'll live. Doubt you'll see him again. He comes back, he'll face a "desertion in the face of the enemy" charge, even though the war's over. Those things are never forgotten – or forgiven.' He turned to Haviland. 'Long way to come to deliver an order, Mr Haviland.'

'Wha—? Oh, I see.' The man was sweating and licked his lips as he glanced at Beth, who kept looking beyond Gunn's shoulder, as if expecting a posse or a bounty hunter to appear. 'Er – well – I am making a delivery, but not of my usual kind,' Haviland said awkwardly, still looking at Beth.

'Finish what you were telling me, Mr Haviland. I'm sure Mr Gunn will be very interested.'

'Yes, of course. Er. . . .' Haviland cleared his throat, put a hand into his vest pocket and brought out something that glittered in the sunlight. Gunn frowned slightly: it was the size of a silver dollar, although the colour was wrong – kind of yellow, like pale gold.

'What that? Some kinda coin?'

'Not a coin, Zack,' Beth said quickly. 'It's a medallion.'

'A trade medallion,' Haviland said. 'Some places back East give these away to advertise their products, usually with a few cents' discount when you make a purchase. Quite effective. I recall one health pill product that—'

'What about *this* particular medallion?' cut in Gunn. 'Why bother bringing it all the way out here to Beth?'

'Mr Haviland was looking for you, Zack.'

Gunn smiled wryly. 'Why would I be interested?'

Beth threw him a sharp look but the storekeeper said, 'See this? On the other side of the medallion there's a quite detailed engraving of a ship under full sail, in big seas. You can make out the figurehead, though it isn't too clear what it's meant to be. But the word "figurehead" is what counts. It's the name of the company that distributes these things and the products they advertise: their motto is "Figurehead – Always Out Front'. Quite appropriate.'

'Nice-looking ship,' Gunn allowed slowly.

'Yes, and to a sailor it would be attractive enough to

make into a medallion to wear around the neck.'

'I still don't. . . . Wait! Josh showed me somethin' like this – his luckpiece! Said it never let him down.'

'I was about to say that Josh Creedy was an ex-mariner. He'd "swallowed the anchor" I believe is the expression when a sailor gives up the sea to live ashore.'

Gunn frowned and Beth said, 'Josh Creedy always wore that medallion around his neck, Zack. He was a bit of a joker in his way, told everyone it was gold, but, of course, it's only brass. Mr Haviland found it outside his store.'

'Just where you had that – er – scuffle with Creedy and that drunken lout, Devlin.'

Gunn's frown deepened. 'Well, it could've been lost during the brawl, I suppose, but Josh was dead by then!' He glanced from the storekeeper to Beth. 'I only glimpsed that medallion in Boulder, so Creedy or Devlin must've had it with him and dropped it during the fight.'

Haviland said, 'Josh Creedy told me he never took it off except to clean it. He bought polish regularly from me to keep it gleaming.' He turned the coin between his stubby fingers now and the sun blazed from it in a golden flash. 'See, he told anyone who was silly enough to listen that it was a gold medal awarded to him for bravery in the Navy during the war.'

'Don't you see, Zack?' Beth said earnestly. 'The only way anyone could get that medallion off Josh was if he was too weak to resist . . . or dead.'

'If you're right, and it was dropped by either Creedy or Devlin during the brawl, then one of them could've killed Josh and taken it off him.'

'It's the only way, Zack!' Beth said excitedly. 'They'll have to drop the charges against you with this evidence, and wh . . . why're you shaking your head like that?'

'Beth, it might've been evidence lying on the ground where I fought with Creedy and Devlin, but here – well, it could've been picked up anywhere.' Haviland drew himself up indignantly and Gunn held up a hand. 'Not accusin' you of anything, storekeeper, just thinking how Murray or Judge Holman will see it.'

Haviland heaved a sigh. 'Unfortunately, I believe you're right.'

Then there was a sudden commotion in the barn. All three swung that way. Gunn quickly lifted the Henry as one big door crashed open and two struggling men appeared, one trying to beat the other's head with his six-gun, while that man flailed, trying to protect himself.

They were Creedy and Devlin, the latter staggering, almost falling. But he regained his balance precariously, drew his pistol and fired at Creedy, who slammed against the barn wall, fumbling his own gun out. He shot across his body. Devlin stumbled to his knees and, as Creedy lumbered forward and kicked him in the ribs, Gunn yelled to the storekeeper: 'Get Beth inside.'

Devlin, on his knees now, fired at Creedy who jumped back, landed crouching, shooting in return. As Gunn turned quickly away the obese storekeeper moved with surprising speed, and thrust the startled Beth inside.

Then Gunn dived for the ground and fired the Henry one-handed, not aimed; the shot was meant only as a distraction. He rolled away, levering in another shell before flopping on to his side. He winced as bullets from both

Creedy's and Devlin's guns gouged the ground beside him, flung gravel and dirt against his body.

He heard Beth cry out his name, then bounded to his feet as the killers started off at a staggering run, separating, forcing him to choose his target. Gunn dropped to one knee, brought down Creedy, who was making for the cover of a water butt. The man's left leg kicked out awkwardly and then he was rolling and skidding through the dust, bringing up against the butt with a jar that knocked the breath from him.

Gunn twisted, levering again. Devlin was struggling to get between the corral bars, one leg still this side of the low rail. There was panic mixed with fear on his face. He triggered a wild burst, emptying his gun without one of the bullets coming even close to Zack.

Gunn fired and the man was slammed violently against the rails, his body tumbling, hanging by one arm. A ribbon of blood dripped from the bottom bar.

Gunn had kept moving all the time. He was close to the barn now, ran to a position where he could see past the half-open door. Creedy had crawled behind the water butt and was just straightening, with his smoking gun lifting. As he fired, the gun wavering, Gunn triggered.

His shot struck sparks from an iron stave and he kicked the big door open wider. He went in, crouching, rifle covering Creedy who was now writhing on the ground. The man's bloody hand was pressed into his right side under his ribcage, his face grey and twisted in pain.

'You – might's well – finish it!' he gasped.

Gunn lowered the rifle hammer and shook his head.

'Not till you do some talking.'

'Go – to – hell!'

'Not yet. What were you and Devlin doing in here?' Gunn casually prodded Creedy in the ribs with the rifle barrel.

Creedy snorted, baring his teeth as a spasm of pain gripped him. 'Figured you'd – show up here – sooner or later.'

Gunn accepted that. 'Why the hell were you and Devlin trying to kill each other?'

The question seemed to rally Creedy and he spat. 'That son of a bitch – killed Josh! My brother! For a chunk of brass any fool could see wasn't gold. . . .' He gurgled and fell back, unconscious.

Then Beth spoke from the doorway. 'Zack! Devlin's still alive, but bleeding badly. Can you lend a hand?'

As Gunn followed the girl to where Devlin was stretched out in the shade of the barn, he asked, 'Did you hear what Creedy said?'

'That Devlin killed Josh? Yes. Oh, Zack, you'll be cleared now and—'

'Only if Devlin lives long enough to admit it.'

She looked sharply at his serious face, then nodded slowly.

'How bad is it?' Gunn asked, looking down at the corpselike Devlin. Haviland glanced up, clutching a handful of bloody rags.

He shook his head. 'I'm no doctor, but he's bleeding terribly.' He indicated the torn flesh that was pulsing bright-red blood. 'It's the exit wound, almost three times the size of the entry hole.'

'All we can do is pack it tightly with rags. We'd better use your buckboard to get him into town.'

'Of course,' agreed the storekeeper readily. 'What about Creedy? Is he still alive?'

'For now,' Gunn told him grimly. 'We'll bring him with us. But even if we've found Josh's killer, I'm not sure it's going to do me any good. Not if they don't live long enough to admit it.'

Doctor Howe called in an associate who happened to be visiting Climax at this time, a friend from medical school days, now a renowned surgeon, having developed swift, life-saving techniques – of necessity – during the war. His name was Phillip Mandrell. He was a cadaverous-looking man, with a heavy moustache that seemed to be eternally twitching. It was disconcerting when he spoke, but Beth and Gunn and the hovering Haviland understood him all right.

'I believe I can go in, Lucas, and reach the source of the problem,' he told Howe, ignoring the anxious trio looking down at Devlin, who more than ever resembled a man with Boot Hill the next stop. 'If you still have those marvellous instruments you brought from Ireland so long ago? Yes, of course, you have. I'll have to be quick. No time to wait for full anaesthesia, but a sniff or two of chloroform should work. It *had* to on the battlefield. He has a partially severed artery spurting all that blood. If I can reach it, I believe my fingers are still nimble enough to tie it off, temporarily at least.'

'If anyone can do it, Phillip, it is you,' said Howe, obviously a fan of Mandrell. 'People, I'll have to ask you

151

please to vacate the room, right now.'

In the small parlour Mrs Howe brought them coffee and biscuits. No one really felt hungry, but the coffee was sure welcome.

'How long's he gonna take?' Gunn asked of nobody in particular.

He started slightly when Beth put out a hand and squeezed his forearm lightly. 'Try to be patient, Zack. I don't think anyone knows we're here. We arrived just on dark and. . . .'

He nodded, tense, paced the small room once or twice. Haviland wanted to return to his wife but Beth pointed out that if he drove his bloodstained buckboard to his store, it was bound to be seen, for this was a Friday, the one night he stayed open for late trading before the weekend.

'Think I'll go check on Creedy.'

Gunn stood and was halfway across the room before Beth could speak. He went out and into the small ante-room where Creedy had been given pain killers by Howe. The man was sleeping, his wounds had been bandaged – they had been severe enough to stop him in his tracks, but the medico dismissed them as non-life-threatening.

Glazed eyes were half-open, but they seemed to focus on Gunn standing beside the bed. Creedy was semicon-scious at best: it was obvious it would be no use questioning him right now. Gunn, disappointed, returned to Beth and Haviland.

He had heard metal instruments clanging in the surgery, a groan or two that probably came from Devlin, but he refrained from opening the door to see how things were progressing.

'Creedy's still out,' he reported to the others. 'He looks a heap better than Devlin, but it's Devlin I need to get me off the hook.'

'I take it you're not a religious man?' Haviland said tentatively; at Gunn's shake of his head he added, 'I do believe this is one of those situations where a prayer might be in order.'

'Deal me out, Mr Haviland,' Gunn said shortly. 'I've never bothered the Almighty, no matter what trouble I was in. Brought up to take care of myself and be responsible for my actions.'

'Very commendable,' Beth said slowly. 'But perhaps Mr Haviland's right. . . ?'

'I got no objections. Just feel that if I got problems they're of my own making, so it's up to me to fix 'em.'

Beth smiled a little as she stared at him, then the connecting door opened and the blood-spattered figure of Dr Mandrell stood there, wiping his red hands on a towel.

'Success, my friends. No guarantee that the patient will live, of course – the difficult I do immediately, but . . . miracles?' He smiled and shrugged. 'They take a little longer. Dr Haviland has sent his daughter to Reconstruction headquarters to bring back a reliable witness for any confession Mr Devlin may make. I say! What. . . ?'

Gunn had his Remington in his hand, cocked, pointed at the medic.

'Zack!' cried Beth in alarm.

'Judas Priest, Doc!' Gunn breathed, voice shaky.

'That's the last goddamn thing I need! They've got a bounty on me! I'm under sentence of death.'

'So I'm told,' Dr Mandrell said in a remarkably calm voice. 'That's exactly why we sent for an acceptable witness. It will surely get your sentence removed post-haste.'

Gunn looked around a little wildly. 'God knows I need Devlin's confession, but I want it all cut and dried with you folk to back me up, rather than have Murray or Killen standing by with a gun against my spine!'

'My dear fellow! I'm so sorry. We thought it wise to have someone in authority standing by to hear what Mr Devlin has to say because – well, he will live a little longer but I can't promise just how long.'

'Zack, I'm sure Dr Howe and Dr Mandrell have only done what they think is best.'

Gunn nodded grimly, not really seeing Beth, his mind racing. He gave a start as he realized he still held a cocked pistol on the surgeon, and he holstered the Remington. 'Thanks, Doc. Sorry I jumped on you, but—'

'No need for apologies. We acted hastily, but doctors are mainly concerned with their patients and—'

'Forget it, Doc,' Gunn said brusquely. Then, turning to Beth, 'I'm gonna have to get out of here. If it's OK, I'll go back to your place and when it's safe you can get word to me. Or, if things go wrong and Devlin doesn't confess, I'll just have to go back on the dodge.'

She looked concerned and went to stand beside him, but he looked towards the door. 'I'll have to go!'

He turned to the nearest door: it was the one that led

to the room where Creedy had been sedated. As Gunn wrenched it open he jumped back in alarm, right hand streaking across his body towards the Remington. But a wild-eyed Creedy swung the six-gun he held – a massive, heavy Colt Dragoon, and Gunn staggered, fell to one knee. Creedy's boot drove into his ribs, knocking him on to his side. Beth cried out and lunged for the half-crazy man.

'Hey, swee'heart!' slurred Creedy, still partially under the effects of the chloroform. 'Jus' what I need!'

One big hand grabbed the startled girl around the waist and pulled her in tightly in front of him. Gunn froze with his pistol half-drawn. The others stared, Haviland making a swift sign of the cross, lips murmuring some prayer, calling for divine intervention.

'Heavens, man,' said Dr Mandrell, who seemed coolest of them all. 'With the amount of anaesthetic I gave you, you should have slept through until morning!'

'Not me, Doc. That stuff never takes with me. Killed a dentist once when it wore off while he was drillin' a tooth. Where you got that sonuver Devlin? All I wanna do is put a slug in him. Reckon I can hang on that long.' He paused, breathless, grimaced, and added, 'Josh – raised me from when I – was eight years old, after Pa – Uh-uh!' he rapped suddenly as Gunn started to take a step closer. He placed the Dragoon's muzzle against Beth's head. 'Made a mi – mishtake. Forgot. Settle wi' you first. Like – righ' now!'

He blinked, pushed Beth to one side and swung the massive Dragoon towards Gunn. Zack dropped to one knee, the Remington sliding into his hand firmly and bucked against his wrist as he got off two swift shots – both drowned out by the thunder of the Dragoon as Creedy managed to fire it.

Zack was picked up as if yanked by a rope. He skidded across the room to bring up with a jar that shook the wall; the smoking gun fell from his hand.

Creedy stood there, the heavy Dragoon down at his side, eyes almost crossed, mouth slack as blood dribbled over his heavy bottom lip. Beth screamed and Creedy dropped to his knees with a thud, leaned sideways and curled up as if he was taking a nap. But he had fallen into a much deeper and longer sleep from which he would never awake.

Beth Landis set down the coffee pot and passed the filled cup across the small table to the man seated opposite. His left arm was in a sling and a bandage partly showed at the open neck of his shirt.

She gestured at a dust cloud coming closer; the riders were dark, bobbing shapes at its base as they headed towards the cabin.

'You know who that is, of course.'

A pale and drawn Zack Gunn sipped his coffee and nodded slowly. 'Murray. Come to kick the dog when it's down.'

'I don't think Murray is quite that bad, Zack,' she said with a mild laugh.

Gunn winced as he moved a little too quickly and the pain in his left shoulder and upper chest caught him like a hatchet blade turning within him. 'Those damn Dragoons! They ought to mount 'em on a carriage and they could use them as artillery!'

'Dr Howe is upset that Creedy was able to get the gun. It belonged to his youngest son who was killed in the war. They kept all his things, just as the Army returned them, in that room. It used to belong to his son. Unfortunately, the items included that Dragoon pistol, fully loaded.'

She fussed with him a little as the riders came nto the yard, seven of them, five troopers, Lieutenant Killen and Major Murray.

She had set up the table on the shady side of the cabin, to the left of the warped front door. Murray halted his men and leaned forward with hands resting on his saddle horn, looking coldly at both Beth and Gunn.

'You have the luck of the Irish, Gunn, or whoever you are. Though I hear you are of Scottish extraction.'

'Long time back, Major. Er – don't let us keep you. Water your horses and be on your way before that rain squall hangin' over the range hits.'

Killen growled like a dog, glanced at Murray, who glared, then smiled slowly.

'Things haven't worked out too bad for you, have they? You may not remember some of them, but perhaps it's better you don't.' He held up a hand as Gunn made to speak. 'Too bad you had to be a lousy Reb. If we'd had a battalion like you the war would've been over a lot earlier.'

'Me a damn Yankee? Not likely!'

'You talk politely to the major, damn you!' snapped Killen, but Murray merely sighed, sober now.

'Well, you're officially a free man now, Gunn. Caught the judge in a right good mood. He'd not only hit a record jackpot playing roulette at a Washington gaming house, but he'd just been told he was a congressman-elect – bound for a governorship in the near future, I'd say.'

'Lucky him. You know he had no choice but to drop the charges agin me,' Gunn said. 'Devlin made his confession. How he put the bite on Josh Creedy, because he thought Josh'd won a big stake at poker. When Josh refused, Devlin was drunk enough to attack him and, well, you know the rest.'

Murray stared, obviously not happy with having to carry out this duty. 'I was you, Gunn, I'd be mighty thankful and I'd clear this neck of the woods mighty soon.' He added curtly, 'Like within two days.'

'Not that soon,' Gunn said, looking sadly at Beth. Then he shrugged. 'Guess that front door don't get fixed after all.'

The major and his men were puzzled but Beth seemed to savvy Gunn's words. And when it became obvious there was to be no further explanation, they took a curt farewell and rode away quickly. No one bothered looking back. No one waved them off.

As their dust settled Beth began to lightly massage his neck and shoulder muscles. 'Doctor's orders, Zack. What did you mean about the front door?'

'Told you it drives me nuts, way it drags across and leans to one side. Don't worry, I'll fix it somehow before I go.'

She stiffened. 'You are leaving, then?'

He squeezed her free hand. 'I still dunno who I am, Beth. Rowan says my name's Bryce McCall. Whether it is or not, it seems I come from Laredo, so that's where I'll start looking. But I'll wait just long enough so I can fix that damn door first!'

She was quiet for a time, then said, a little breathlessly, 'Oh, leave the damn door as it is!'

'With winter coming on, and. . . ?'

'If you fix it before you go you won't have any excuse for – for coming back,' she said with a rush, bosom heaving, a catch in her voice.

He stared up at her as she moved around in front of him. He reached for her with his good arm and pulled her into his lap, careful not to bump his bad arm.

'To hell with the door. I don't need *that* for an excuse to come back.'

It took but a moment for her to realize what he meant.

Then she laughed, but the sound was quickly muffled as his mouth covered hers.